...ecause she used to ...
...otion. "I wore too much fragrance."

"Not to me."

...nstantly, she was reminded of him burying his nose
...n her sugary skin. Oh, the memories that invoked:
...urling up in Ryan's bed when his dad wasn't home,
...ipping her greedy hands into his half-undone clothes,
...osing her eyes while he peeled hers off. Even now,
...er eyes were starting to drift closed, until she realized
...at Ryan was looking at her.

...e told herself to get a grip. But it didn't work. She
...uldn't get her memories under control. "I think I
...ould go now."

...made a puzzled expression. "Go?"

...o my room. To get some work done." She needed
...scape. If she didn't, those intimate feelings would
...y get stronger.

...e walked away, praying for the strength to make it
...rough the rest of the week without feeling more for
him than she should.

LOST AND FOUND FATHER

BY
SHERI WHITEFEATHER

All the characters in this book have no existence outside the imagination of the author, and have no relation whatsoever to anyone bearing the same name or names. They are not even distantly inspired by any individual known or unknown to the author, and all the incidents are pure invention.

© Sheri WhiteFeather 2013

ISBN: 978 0 263 90145 0

Harlequin (UK) policy is to use papers that are natural, renewable and recyclable products and made from wood grown in sustainable forests. The logging and manufacturing processes conform to the legal environmental regulations of the country of origin.

Printed and bound in Spain
by Blackprint CPI, Barcelona

MILLS BOON

First published in Great Britain 2013
by Mills & Boon, an imprint of Harlequin (UK) Limited,
Eton House, 18-24 Paradise Road, Richmond, Surrey TW9 1SR

© Sheree Henry-Whitefeather 2013

ISBN: 978 0 263 90145 0
ebook ISBN: 978 1 472 00533 5

23-0913

Harlequin
recyclable
logging ar
regulation

Printed ar
by Blackp

Sheri WhiteFeather is a bestselling author who has won numerous awards, including readers' and reviewers' choice honors. She writes a variety of romance novels for Mills & Boon. She has become known for incorporating Native American elements into her stories. She has two grown children who are tribally enrolled members of the Muscogee Creek Nation.

Sheri is of Italian-American descent. Her great-grandparents immigrated to the United States from Italy through Ellis Island, originating from Castel di Sangro and Sicily. She lives in California and enjoys ethnic dining, shopping in vintage stores and going to art galleries and museums. Sheri loves to hear from her readers. Visit her website at www.SheriWhiteFeather.com.

Chapter One

Ryan's past had come back to haunt him. But it had always been there, chipping away at his soul.

He glanced at the clock. Victoria was on her way to see him. Yes, *that* Victoria. The girl with whom he'd fathered a child. They'd dated steadily during their sophomore and junior years in high school, and they'd been crazy about each other. But after she got pregnant, everything fell apart.

Two sixteen-years-olds scared beyond belief.

Although Victoria couldn't bear to terminate the pregnancy, keeping the baby wasn't an option, either. Her parents convinced her that adoption was the answer. Ryan's dad was equally adamant. Under no circumstances should Ryan become a teenage father.

An open adoption was discussed, but both families thought that a closed adoption was more suitable and would make the situation easier for everyone.

Soon an ultrasound revealed that the baby was a girl. Victoria cried all of the time, and Ryan walked around in a daze. Although their relationship started to unravel, they agreed to hold their daughter, just once, to say goodbye to her together.

Only when the time came, Ryan panicked and never showed up at the hospital. A decision that tore him and Victoria apart for good. After that, she refused to speak to him. And rightly so. He'd spurned her when she'd needed him most.

He couldn't fathom how many times over the years he'd thought about Victoria and the baby, or how badly he'd regretted his decision. It had even interfered with his marriage. But Ryan didn't want to go there. He didn't want to think about that.

So what did he want to think about?

The day Victoria had moved away? After the baby was born, her parents had relocated to Los Angeles to give Victoria a fresh start. And now she was back in Oregon for the sole purpose of knocking at his front door.

Cripes, he was nervous.

Last week she'd called and told him about Kaley, making him an expectant father all over again.

Apparently, six months ago, Victoria had contacted numerous adoption-reunion registries, hoping to find their daughter. Swiftly and miraculously, she had. Kaley, their eighteen-year-old daughter, had contacted some of the same registries, trying to locate her birth parents.

According to Victoria, she and Kaley had gotten quite close. They'd formed a strong and steady bond. And now Kaley wanted to meet him, too.

He was humbled and downright awed by his daughter's interest in him. But it wasn't happening today. Victoria wanted to see him first, to evaluate his sincerity, no doubt. He couldn't blame her for being cautious, not after what he'd done.

A snorting sound caught his attention, and he shifted his gaze to the bulldog curled up in the corner. If he didn't know better, he would've thought the dog was mocking him. Beside the bulldog was a border collie, fast asleep. Ryan had a scatter of farm animals, too, that had more or less come with the house.

He lived in an old farmhouse, surrounded by woods. On the same property was a carriage house that served as his veterinary clinic.

He checked the clock again. Victoria was late.

What if she changed her mind? What if she left him hanging? No, he thought. She wouldn't do that. She would follow through for their daughter's sake.

Still, she'd been reluctant to discuss Kaley at length over the phone. He hadn't even seen a picture. He'd asked Victoria to email a photo, but she said that she would bring some with her.

He had all sorts of questions about Kaley. He wondered about Victoria, too. For all he knew she was married with other kids. Her husband might even be coming with her. He hadn't queried her about her relationship status, and she hadn't offered the information. He could have searched for her on Google to see what came up, but that would have made him feel like a stalker, so he'd let it be.

As for himself, he'd told her that he was divorced and lived alone, letting her know there wasn't anyone, aside from him, for Kaley to meet. Even Ryan's dad was gone. He'd died a few years back. During the course of their limited conversation, she'd said she was sorry for his loss, and he'd asked about her parents, to which she'd replied, "They're fine." No other details were discussed.

As he waited, his nervousness ratcheted up a notch. He didn't know what to do with himself. He was afraid that he would screw up again somehow, say the wrong thing, do the wrong thing. He wanted so badly to make it up to Victoria. He hoped that she didn't show up with a husband or significant other. Having another man there would infringe on the moment.

Infringe on what moment? What was he expecting out of this, for Victoria to hug him and say it was okay? That she understood that he was just a kid back then? That was a lame excuse, and he damned well knew it. She'd been young and scared, too.

Maybe he *should* have searched for her on Google. He would feel a whole lot better right now if he'd seen a recent picture of her on a social networking site or wherever. At least then she might not seem like as much of a stranger. He tried to envision how she was going to look today, but he drew a blank. All he could see was the sweet girl from his mixed-up youth. The girl whose peppermint kisses used to set his libido on fire, the girl—

Ding-dong.

The doorbell chimed, and he nearly leaped out of his skin. The dogs jumped up and barked, intensifying the frenzied feeling. He expelled the air in his lungs and hushed them.

He answered the door and came face-to-face with Victoria. She was by herself, and she looked the same yet different. Her eyes were just as green, her complexion was just as fair, and her hair was the same fiery copper shade of red, only she wore it sleek and straight instead of in a riot of curls. The waiflike girl had become a sophisticated woman. Attired in a slim-fitting dress and high-heeled sandals, she boasted L.A. chic.

His pulse pounded something fierce. He couldn't stop staring, which was a totally improper thing to do. But she was staring at him, too. He'd matured as dramatically as she had. He was no longer a lanky boy. He stood before her as a rough-edged man with frown lines at the corners of his eyes.

Breaking the silence, he said, "Come on in."

"Thank you." Her voice was as polished as her appearance.

As she crossed the threshold, the dogs waggled at her feet. They were trained not to jump on guests, but he could tell that they wanted to paw her.

Victoria smiled, but not at Ryan. She was acknowledging the canines. Nonetheless, her smile struck familiarity, leaving him with a pang in the pit of his stomach.

When she lifted her head, their gazes met and held once again. She glanced away first, and Ryan battled a string of emotion. Unable to curb his curiosity, he stole a peek at her left hand, which bore no trace of a ring. But that didn't mean she wasn't in a committed relationship. He would do well to remember that.

"Have a seat." He gestured to the living room, which was furnished with rustic pieces and minimal clutter.

Victoria sat in a leather chair. Had she avoided the sofa so he couldn't sit next to her? He suspected that beneath the L.A. chic she was as nervous as he was. This couldn't be any easier for her than it was for him, being in the same room with the guy who'd left her alone at the hospital.

Before he forgot his manners, he asked, "Would you like something to drink? I've got water, of course, and orange juice in the fridge. Or I can make a pot of coffee."

"No, thanks, I'm fine."

He moved forward and sat on the edge of the sofa, uncomfortable in his own home. He was still attracted to her, and he had no right to be. "Did you bring the pictures of Kaley?"

Victoria nodded and opened her purse. She extended an envelope toward him.

He took it from her, and soon he was studying a young woman with familiar features. Kaley had inherited Victoria's refined nose and full mouth, but her dark hair, deep-set eyes and tanned complexion favored his.

Overwhelmed by her image, his heart did a daddy-in-waiting flip. "She's beautiful."

Pride colored Victoria's voice. "And smart, too. She's starting college in the fall, and she's going to major in business, with a minor in women's studies."

He glanced at the pictures again. He didn't know what women's studies entailed, other than a connection to feminism, but he was eager to know more about Kaley's interest in it and what sort of career she envisioned. "Where at?"

"UCLA. She was raised in L.A. All of these years she was close by, and I didn't even know it."

Ryan's whereabouts put him hundreds of miles away from the reunion loop. "When am I going to get to meet her?"

Victoria shifted in her chair. "Are you sure you're ready? That you won't back out at the last minute?"

He deserved that. If he were in her shoes, he would

have said the same thing. But it still stung. "I've grown up since we last saw each other."

"I'm aware of how old you are."

"I wasn't talking about my chronological age, Tore."

"Yes, but time doesn't necessarily change people." Her voice cracked a little. "And please don't call me Tore."

The vulnerability in her tone shamed him. He hadn't meant to use his old nickname for her. He hadn't meant for it to slip so easily from his tongue.

"I'm sorry," he said, knowing those words did little or nothing to absolve him. "I don't want to make this any harder than it already is. But I *have* changed, and I want to get to know my daughter." He would come through this time.

A beat of painful silence passed before she responded, "I'm glad that you want to get to know her, but there's a lot to consider. Kaley is searching for missing links in her identity. This is as much about her as it is about you."

He braved the question he hated to address. "Does she know about me not showing up at the hospital?"

"No. She's inquisitive about the past, but that isn't something I was able to summon the strength to tell her."

Because old wounds ran deep, he thought, wishing he could comfort Victoria somehow.

She quietly added, "She asked me about the day she was born. If I saw her before the adoption agency took her away. I told her that I did and that I held her, too."

"She didn't ask about me?"

Victoria shook her head. "I think she automatically assumed you were part of it since you were my boyfriend at the time and not just some random guy who made me pregnant."

That made him feel worse. "Do you think I should tell her the truth?"

Her tone remained quiet. "That's up to you."

"I think I should." He just hoped that he could explain his actions in way that made sense. Even after all of these years, he couldn't quite define his panic, aside from him being a teenage boy who'd been afraid to face the final countdown.

Would that reason be enough for Kaley?

Anxious to know more about her and how she was raised, he asked, "What are her adoptive parents like?"

"Her mother passed away about seven years ago. From what I understand, she was an amazing woman. Kaley's identity quest has a lot to do with her."

His heart went out to his daughter. His mother died when he was a kid, too. "And the dad?"

"Eric is a wonderful father. They're extremely close. He supports her in every way. I've become close to him, too."

He felt a stab of envy, but he said, "That's good."

Victoria continued by saying, "He's half-Native, like you are. Kaley doesn't look adopted. She looks as if she could be his. She even speaks a little Cherokee. That's the tribe he's from."

He was still holding pictures of the child he'd helped create. The child another man had nurtured. Apparently Eric was ingrained in his roots. Ryan didn't know much his about Native side. In his case, it was Paiute. But he'd been raised by his Anglo father. "I expected Kaley to have at least one Native parent." There was a federal act that stipulated that Native babies were supposed to be adopted within their culture. "It's nice that she speaks some Cherokee."

"She speaks Spanish, too. She took it all through high school. She's good with languages."

"I'd really like to meet her, and I swear I'll do my best not to disappoint her."

Victoria studied him from across the coffee table, and he absorbed her scrutiny, all the way to his anxious soul.

After an audible breath, she conceded. "She'll be out of school soon on summer break next week. We can figure something out then."

"That would be great. I'd love for her to visit. Maybe she could stay for a week or so. You could come with her, if that would make her more comfortable. In fact, you could both stay here."

Her eyes went wide. "*Here?* In your house?"

"Why not? I've got plenty of room. Besides, the nearest motel is clear out on the highway, as you well know. My house is more convenient." He chanced an intimate remark, needing to know, needing to mention it. "If you have a significant other, you can invite him, too."

She lifted her chin in what struck him as false bravado. He waited to see what her answer would be, a look of shattered innocence pulsing between them.

Then she said, "I'm not involved with anyone. I prefer being single."

He told himself that her status didn't matter. Nor did her uneasy claim. In spite of his attraction to her, he wasn't trying to rekindle anything except the parenthood they'd lost. But he was still glad that she was single. "What about your job?"

"What about it?" she parroted.

"Would you be able to get the time off?"

"I'm a web designer." She clasped her hands on her lap, a bit too properly. "I have my own company."

He pressed the issue. He couldn't help it. Now that he'd opened the let's-be-parents-together door, he wasn't about to close it. "Then you should bring Kaley and the two of you should stay here. If she's willing, of course. If not, I'll go to California to meet her."

"Personally I don't think staying here is a good idea, but I'll talk to her about it. She's an adult, and she can make her own decisions."

"Okay. Thanks." What else could he say? What else could he do but wait for the outcome? He'd already given it his best.

"I should go. I'm flying back tonight." She stood up and collected her purse.

He didn't want her to leave. He wanted to make everything right, to fix what he'd broken, to see forgiveness in her eyes. But he couldn't stop her from leaving any more than she could have stopped him from running away all those years ago.

He walked her onto the porch and down the stairs, where they stood in the sun. The air was perfumed with flowering foliage, and it reminded him of the wild ginger they used to pick. Everything had seemed wild then, including the inexperienced love they'd made.

He turned to look at her and caught her watching him. She'd gone vulnerable again. She was twisting the ends of her hair, an anxious habit he recognized from their youth.

She said, "I'll get back to you after I talk to Kaley."

"I'll be waiting for your call." He tucked his hands

into his jean pockets. Was that his anxious teenage habit? "Have a safe trip home."

"Thank you." She quit twisting her hair, but she was still discomposed.

Clearly, the memories between them had become palpable. He didn't doubt that Victoria felt it, too.

They said goodbye, and he watched her walk to her rental car. She didn't glance back at him, and he didn't remove his hands from his pockets or return to his big, empty house until she was gone.

Victoria was home. Her plane had touched down last night, and this morning she was a bundle of nerves.

She glanced around her apartment. Decorated with carefully selected furniture and contemporary artwork, it depicted her California lifestyle, right down to the luxurious poolside view.

Ryan's house depicted his lifestyle, too. The red-and-white farmhouse suited him, and so did the shingle out front.

Carriage House Veterinary Care. Ryan Nash, DVM.

He'd attained his country-boy dream. He'd always wanted to be a vet, and he'd set up practice in his hometown. Her former hometown. A place she'd never intended to see again.

Because of him.

He looked considerably different from the boy she'd known. He was bigger and broader, but his face was much more angular. Those killer cheekbones were totally lethal now, and so was the concentration in his stone-brown eyes.

She'd tried so hard to compose herself while she'd been there, but she hadn't done as well as she'd hoped.

Her heart had been thudding the entire time and her stupid voice had cracked.

Was Ryan genuinely sorry for the past? Was he mature enough to handle a relationship with Kaley? He seemed to be. But that didn't ease the old ache. She'd loved Ryan. He'd been her everything, and on the day he'd left her alone with the baby they'd created, he'd reduced her to nothing. It taken her years to get over him, and she'd been careful to avoid any news of him, staying as far away as possible. But now, God help her, she was being drawn back in.

She walked onto the balcony, coffee in hand, and blew out a breath. She'd called Kaley earlier and told the anxious teenager that she was back from her trip, but she hadn't mentioned Ryan's invitation for both of them to go to Oregon. She would be meeting Kaley for lunch, where she going to delve into the specifics.

If only Victoria could relax; if only he hadn't rattled her once-broken heart. The really pathetic thing was that she was wondering about his ex, who she was, if the divorce had been her idea, if he missed being married.

When Victoria first discovered that she was pregnant, she'd dreamed of Ryan proposing to her. Young and naive, she'd actually believed that they could make a marriage work, even if it meant waiting until they were eighteen. She'd mapped it out in her mind, how they could live with their parents and raise the baby between both households. Then, once they were married, Ryan could get a loan for college and secure their future.

But he didn't propose, and she didn't tell him about her marriage dreams. She'd never told him that she loved him, either. After they'd agreed to give up the baby, her only consolation was that he'd promised to be there when their daughter was born.

And the rest, as the saying went, was history.

Before her thoughts drove her into a deeper sense of painful distraction, she finished her coffee and went into the bathroom to take a long, invigorating shower.

By the time she emerged, her skin was flushed and her hair was damp and starting to misbehave. She put on a robe and plugged in the blow-dryer and flatiron, preparing to use both devices. Once she tamed her curls, she applied makeup and got dressed.

Ready to greet the afternoon and see her daughter, she drove to the sushi bar they favored.

Victoria arrived first and sat in the cramped waiting area. About five minutes later, Kaley walked in wearing denim shorts, a pastel-printed T and rhinestone flip-flops. Her hair streamed down her back, and with her golden tan and welcoming smile, she was a lovely sight to behold.

As they embraced, the teenager said, "Hey, Victoria."

She didn't expect Kaley to call her Mom, but on occasion Kaley referred to her as *mi otra madre,* which meant "my other mother" in Spanish. It was a reference that made Victoria feel like the most privileged woman on earth.

A hostess seated them, and they sat across from each other at a small table near the window. Water was delivered, and they studied their menus, energy buzzing between them.

"How did it go?" Kaley eagerly asked.

Such a loaded question, Victoria thought, but she did her best to respond in a positive way. "Ryan is anxious to meet you."

"I'm excited about meeting him, too." The child she'd conceived with him leaned closer. "What's he like?"

"He looks different" was all she could seem to manage. Strong and handsome in a way she hadn't imagined. When she saw that Kaley was waiting for a more in-depth response, she quickly added, "He seems successful." But she'd always believed that he would make a good vet. "He has a nice country home and a couple of cute dogs. But most importantly, he's receptive to having you in his life."

"So what happens now? Is he going to call me? Am I supposed to call him?"

Okay, Victoria thought. *Here goes.* "I offered to call him after you and I talked. He wants you to stay at his house for a week or so. He also invited me to come with you." She paused to collect herself. "But he'll come here if you'd prefer not to go there."

"Oh, wow. Really?" Kaley reached for her water, and the ice clinked in her half-tipped glass. "I'd probably get to know him better if I went there. Don't you think?"

She wanted to discourage her daughter from making the trip, but sitting here gazing at the girl's wistful expression, she couldn't do it. "It's your choice. He's your…" She couldn't bring herself to say "father" or "birth father" or anything that identified him as family, so she let the sentence drift.

"Are you willing to go with me? Or is that totally out of the question?"

Victoria's heartbeat accelerated. "Is that what you want?"

"Are you kidding? I'd be really nervous without you. Besides, I know Dad would feel better if you were there."

The dad she spoke of was Eric, the man who'd shaped her into the amazing young woman she'd become. Victoria would be forever grateful to him. "You're right. He would worry otherwise. And so would I." Expecting Kaley to visit with Ryan for the first time by herself wasn't in the girl's best interest. "I'll go with you."

The teenager fanned herself. "I can't believe this is happening."

Neither could Victoria. She felt as if she were having an out-of-body experience. If someone would've told her that someday she would be sleeping under Ryan's roof with their grown child in tow, she would have deemed that person crazy. Plus Kaley didn't know that Victoria had loved Ryan. No one did.

She looked across the table at her daughter. Every excruciating detail of the day Kaley was born was still imbedded in her mind. While she'd held the swaddled infant, she'd waited desperately for Ryan to show up. She'd also glanced endlessly at her parents, begging them to ask the representative from the adoption agency for more time. But eventually the extra time ran out. The most painful moment was right before they'd taken Kaley away. She'd clutched the baby close to her chest, wishing she could nurse her, wishing she could take her home, with or without Ryan. It was the worst day of her life.

But now she had her daughter back. Kaley meant the world to her, and if making peace with Ryan was part of the deal, then that was what she would do.

Even if being in his company still made her hurt.

Chapter Two

This was it. Victoria and Kaley would be arriving at Ryan's house any minute, he hoped. He'd offered to pick them up at the airport and lend them his truck whenever they needed a vehicle, but Victoria insisted on renting a car.

They would be staying for the equivalent of a week, starting today, which was a bright and sunny Thursday.

He waited on the porch steps. At this point, he didn't care if he appeared anxious, sitting outside the way he was. He needed the fresh air. Besides, he *was* anxious, and no doubt Kaley was, too. He imagined Victoria was as well, but not for the same eager-to-bond reason. She was probably dreading every upcoming second that she'd agreed to spend in Oregon.

His dogs sat beside him, glancing around. From his body language, they obviously sensed that something was up.

A midsize sedan pulled up to the curb, and Ryan jumped to his feet. The dogs followed his lead.

"Behave, you guys," he said.

They looked at him with expectation, as if to ask who was coming to see them.

"My daughter," he automatically replied, heading out to the vehicle. "So make a good impression." He said the latter part as much to himself as to the dogs. He desperately wanted Kaley to like him. Victoria, too, but he didn't know if that was possible.

Kaley got out of the car first, and he lost every ounce of breath in his lungs. He recognized her from her pictures, only she was taller than he'd expected, and in the sun, her long dark hair glinted with hints of auburn. She was more beautiful than anyone he'd ever seen. Because she was his, he thought, wishing for the millionth time that he'd been there when she was born.

They both stood a little awkwardly, gazing at each other. He noticed right away her colorful clothes and bangle bracelets.

Finally, they said hello and reached forward for a hug. He was cautious not to hold her too tightly for fear that he would smother her with his daddy desperation.

"It's so good have you here," he said.

"It's good to be here."

They separated, and he noticed that Victoria had gotten out of the car and was lingering off to the side. He suspected that she was staying in the background deliberately, giving him and Kaley a chance to get acquainted.

The teenager glanced down at the dogs. "Look how adorable you two are." She asked Ryan, "What are their names?"

He smiled, grateful that animals were an icebreaker. "Perky and Pesky."

She laughed. "Let me guess. Perky is the black-and-white one with the bright expression, and Pesky is the chubby guy wiggling for attention." Upon hearing his name, Pesky grinned, flashing his crooked teeth. Kaley laughed again.

Ryan couldn't take his eyes off his daughter. There she was, so grown up, standing right before him and wanting to be part of his life. He longed to hug her again. But he didn't. He knew it would be weird to keep grabbing her.

Victoria came forward, and she and Ryan exchanged a quiet greeting, a simple "Hi" in the presence of the child they'd created. Talk about surreal.

Trying to act casual, he said to Victoria, "If you pop the trunk, I'll get the bags."

"We can help, too," Kaley said. "We brought a lot of stuff. We even bought some new outfits for the trip. But it was just an excuse for us to shop."

"Mall fever," Victoria put in, making Kaley grin.

Ryan didn't mind that they'd over-packed. The more stuff they brought, the more of a vacation it seemed.

Everyone pitched in with the bags. The women had an easy rapport with each other. He was definitely the odd man out, but he'd expected as much.

While they headed for the porch, Pesky stayed close to Kaley. Ryan asked her, "Do you have pets?"

"We have two cats. Dad calls them the bougainvillea babies because when they were kittens, they used to hide in the flowers on our patio. Sometimes Dad calls me a bougainvillea baby, too. He has all sorts of nicknames for me. He says I'm a daddy's girl, like the cats. They're girls, too."

Although Ryan smiled, he struggled with a twinge of envy. He knew that he shouldn't react that way every time her adoptive father was mentioned. If anything, he should be thanking the other man for making her a daddy's girl.

He opened the door, and they went inside.

Kaley glanced around. "Victoria told me how nice she thought this place was." His daughter stepped farther into the living room, where a stone fireplace and woven rugs presided. "I really like it, too."

"Thanks. I bought it about three years ago." He knew his house could use a woman's touch, but he wasn't about to say that. "It was built in the 1800s, but it's obviously been renovated since then." He chanced a daddy's girl remark. "You can be a buttercup baby here. I put some in your room. I picked them in the woods."

"Buttercup baby. Oh, that's cute."

Ryan appreciated her enthusiasm. It was just what he needed. In the silence, he glanced at Victoria, wondering what she was thinking. She was standing on the other side of him.

He said to her, "I put some flowers in your room, too."

She adjusted the strap of her purse, which kept slipping off her shoulder. "You didn't need to pick anything for me."

"I wanted to."

Before things got quiet again, Kaley said, "Can we see your backyard before we see our rooms?"

"Sure." They left the luggage where it was and

headed to the kitchen, which led to the mudroom and back door.

"It's so green and pretty." His daughter was impressed. "And check out the chickens." She laughed and mimicked one of the hens clucking along in the coop. She glanced across the yard at the barn. "Do you have horses?"

"Just one. An old grandpa who needed a home."

"Was he a rescue?"

"In a way, I guess. He belonged to the people who sold me this place, but they couldn't take him where they were going, so I agreed to keep him. He's a draft horse, loyal as can be. I inherited a miniature cow, too. The chickens were also part of the deal."

"I never even knew there were miniature cows. Do you milk it?"

"Yes. I can teach you sometime this week, if you'd like."

"Imagine that—me milking a little cow. That sounds fun."

He smiled, and they returned to the house and finished the indoor tour, where he took the women upstairs to their rooms.

Victoria's was first, a brightly lit space furnished with an oak-framed bed and matching dresser, where the flowers sat. He'd chosen spring beauties for her. The last of the summer blooms. He'd been tempted to add some wild ginger to the bouquet, but he'd refrained, concerned that it would be too blatant a reminder of their youth.

"This is lovely," she said and placed her bags in the corner. "Thank you."

"You're welcome." A beat of emotion passed between

them, something they were obviously going to have to get used to.

When they entered Kaley's room, she beamed over her flowers. She opened her toiletries suitcase and searched around for a bobby pin so she could clip one of the buttercups in her hair.

Once the yellow bloom was in place, she sat on the edge of the bed and asked Ryan, "Do you have any photos around, of your parents or grandparents or anyone? I'm interested in seeing them. Plus I'm starting a family tree, and when I did research about it online, they said to go through old pictures and documents. Victoria has been helping me with her side, and I was hoping you would help me with yours."

He hadn't considered Kaley taking the interest in her roots quite that far, but Victoria warned him that their daughter was on an identity quest, so he should have been better prepared. "There's a box in the attic with that kind of stuff in it. I can get it down tomorrow."

"That would be great. I also have some pictures to show you. I brought a photo album with me in it that my mom made when I was little. You can look through it tomorrow, too, if you want."

"Okay." Still a bit overwhelmed, he marveled at Kaley's easy manner. "Are you hungry? How does pizza sound for dinner tonight? We can order in."

She grinned. "I love pizza."

"So do I," he replied, then addressed Victoria. "You always did, too. Unless your tastes have changed."

Her purse strap fell down again. "I still like it."

"Then that's what we'll get."

Once they decided on the toppings, Kaley stayed in

her room to call her father, and Ryan and Victoria went downstairs to wait for the delivery.

She occupied the leather chair in the living room, leaving him the sofa. She was making a habit of sitting apart from him.

"I'm not much of a cook," he said, struggling for conversation. The beat of emotion that passed between them earlier was getting stronger. "Mostly I fix easy things. Or eat out."

She glanced in the direction of the kitchen, as if she was trying to make their exchange seem more normal. "I don't mind cooking while I'm here. It will give me something to do. But I brought work with me, too."

He forced an easy tone. "I'm taking the week off. My staff is, too. I gave them paid vacations, rather than keep the clinic open while you're visiting. I want to spend as much time with Kaley as I can." Curious about his daughter's culinary skills, he asked, "Does she like to cook?"

"Mostly Kaley and Eric eat out or prepare simple meals, like you do. But I'm going to teach her to bake. She remembers the goodies her mom used to make, and she wants to try her hand at it."

Ryan had been in kindergarten when his mother passed away. His memories of her were practically non-existent. "Maybe the two of you can do some baking while you're here."

"Maybe we can."

Being a new parent was different for Ryan than it was for Victoria because Kaley still had a father. Already he was nervous about the plans they'd made for tomorrow. "My contribution to the family tree will probably suck. My dad never talked about our relatives. I probably won't even know who's who."

"Don't worry about it." She eased his concern. "My side hasn't been all that riveting, either."

"At least your parents are still around."

"Yes, and with the same detached attitude."

Ryan nodded in understanding. Neither of them had come from nurturing homes.

She said, "My parents weren't receptive to the idea of me searching for Kaley. They were worried that it might turn out badly. And now that I found her, they're still not overly supportive. Nor have they made a genuine effort to get to know her or help with the family tree. I think they're still under the belief that adoptions should remain closed."

"I remember how adamant they were about that."

She nodded. "So was your dad."

True, but it wasn't his dad who'd stopped him from going to the hospital. Ryan had made that mistake himself.

"Kaley's mom was adopted."

He blinked, cleared his mind. "Really?"

"Kaley can tell you more about her. Mostly she's the reason that Kaley wanted to find us. I think the family tree was influenced by her, too. Her name was Corrine. There are pictures of her in Kaley's photo album. And some of Eric, too." She paused, as if to collect her thoughts. "Corrine was the love of Eric's life. Sometimes his voice still quavers when he talks about her."

A sense of sadness crept over him. "Are there newborn pictures of Kaley in the album?"

"Yes. The hospital took some and gave them to her parents." Silent, she glanced away.

Ryan suspected that she'd slipped back to being the girl he'd crushed, reliving the moment.

"I'm sorry I hurt you," he said. "If I could change it, I would."

She didn't meet his gaze. "It turned out all right. Kaley is here with us now."

"Yes, but it's still haunting us. You can barely stand to look at me, and I barely know what to say to you."

Defying his comment, she shifted her gaze, staring straight at him. "I've looked at you plenty."

"And you're still seeing me for who I was, not for who I am."

"Please, Ryan. I don't want to dwell on the past. What's done is done, and I accept your apology."

A painful acceptance. Her voice was shaking, making him think of Eric and his dead wife. Had Ryan killed a part of Victoria on the day their daughter was born? Did her hurt go deeper than it should, deeper than a place even Kaley could reach?

With his burden worsening he said, "I think I need to tell Kaley the truth before she shows me the album." If he didn't, he would feel like a fraud, looking at pictures of the infant he should have cradled in his arms. "In fact, I should probably tell her tonight."

"Do you want me leave the room when you explain it to her?"

"God, no. I want you to hear the truth, too." He needed for her to hear it.

"I already know what happened."

"But we never discussed it." Since she'd refused to speak to him after Kaley was born, and he'd been too ashamed to try to make amends, he'd kept his distance. After she moved away, he'd sunk deeper into himself, barely talking to anyone at school. By the time college rolled around, he'd been eager to get out of town and never come back. But after he'd earned his DVM, he'd changed his mind and resumed his life here.

The doorbell rang, signaling the pizza delivery. Grateful for the mental reprieve, Ryan jumped up to answer it.

He paid for the food and put it on the coffee table, along with some paper plates, sodas and napkins. Victoria didn't say anything about his decision to eat in the living room. But that was where he took most of his meals.

Kaley came downstairs, having heard the doorbell, too. Her new best friend, Pesky the bulldog, was following her.

"Pizza looks good," she said.

"Help yourself." He noticed that she still had the buttercup in her hair, making his heart do the daddy thing and skitter around in his chest.

Kaley sat beside him, then took two slices. Victoria chose one, which she picked at, removing the toppings and sampling them first. But she'd always eaten the crust last. She did that with sandwiches, too. As Ryan watched her, he wondered if his memories of her would be as vivid if she was merely his high-school sweetheart and not the mother of his child. Was she cemented in his mind because of Kaley? Or would Victoria have made a lasting impression either way?

He finally turned to Kaley and said, "There's something I need to tell you."

She tilted her head. "About what?"

"The day you were born. I wasn't at the hospital."

She kept the pizza plate on her lap. "How come?"

"Because I couldn't handle it."

"That's okay." She took a casual approach. "A lot of people who give up their babies for adoption think it's easier not to see them."

"There's more to it than that. I promised Victoria that I would be there. I gave her my word, and I had every intention of keeping it. But when the day came, I panicked."

Kaley went silent. Victoria was quiet, too. Both listening to what he had to say.

"It was around five in the morning, and the phone rang, dragging me out of a restless sleep." He'd been restless the entire nine months, aware of every moment of every pregnant day. "My dad answered it, and after he hung up, he came into my room and said that Victoria was in labor."

Kaley brought Victoria directly into conversation. "Was it you who called?"

"No, it was my mother." She didn't elaborate, allowing Ryan to continue.

The scene unfolded in his mind, colorful yet choppy, like patchwork pieces of a torn quilt. "Dad didn't say anything else to me. He left the house to go to work. It was a school day, but he wasn't expecting me to go to school. He assumed that I would take my truck and head over to the hospital, which was what I planned to do. I had an old Ford that he'd overhauled for me. Dad was a mechanic." He mentioned those details because they were part of the memory. "I got ready and went out to my truck with these two little teddy bears that I'd been keeping in my drawer. One was for you and the other one was for Victoria." He shifted his gaze to the mother of his child. "I bought them about a month before. I figured the new parents could give Kaley hers, and I was thinking that you'd keep yours and always know that you had the same toy as our daughter."

She swallowed, as if a lump had just formed in her throat. "What happened to the bears?"

"I kept them for about a year, torturing myself with them, I guess. Then when I went off to college, I donated them to the Goodwill. I didn't know what else to do with them."

"I wish you still had them," Kaley said.

"So do I. Then I could give them to both of you now." Because his mouth had gone dry, he reached for his soda and took a sip. "Not that it would change any of this, though."

"Tell us the rest of your story," Kaley said. "You went out to the truck with the bears. Then what did you do?"

"I got behind the wheel. Then suddenly my heart started racing and I couldn't breathe. I was having a panic attack. At the time, I didn't know that's what it was called, but I knew it was because of the baby. I returned to the house and sat on the sofa, trying to catch my breath and rebuild my courage to go to the hospital. But I never did."

"You stayed in your living room the whole time I was in labor?" Victoria asked.

He nodded. "After a while the phone rang, and I figured it was your mom, calling to see where I was. It rang on and off, all day. When the calls started coming closer together, I assumed that you'd had the baby." He divided his gaze between both of the women in his presence. "The two of you deserved better."

"It didn't affect me," Kaley said. "I don't remember

any of it. But I feel badly for Victoria." She spoke to her birth mom. "That must have been really sad for you."

"It was. But it's done and over now."

"I can tell it still hurts." Kaley glanced over at Ryan. "You look like you're hurting, too."

"I just wish I could go back and redo it the right way."

Kaley made a goofy face. "I can act like a baby if it will make you feel better."

When she stuck her thumb in her mouth, Ryan couldn't help but smile. "Keep that up and I'll to have to buy you another teddy bear."

She removed her thumb with a deliberate pop. "Actually that would be cool. Where'd you buy the first ones?"

"At a discount store on the edge of town."

"Is it still there?"

"Yes."

"Can we go there this week?"

"Sure. We can pick out a new bear together."

"Are you going to get Victoria a new one, too?"

His pulse went jumpy. "If she wants me to." He asked her, "Do you?"

She shrugged, albeit it gently. "It doesn't matter."

"I think you should be included. Then you and Kaley can have the matching toys you were supposed have. We can all go to the store together."

Their daughter chimed in. "You know what else we should all do together? Go to the maternity ward of the hospital. So I can see the place where I was born and so you guys can make new memories."

Ryan loved the idea, especially since Kaley suggested it. But Victoria had to agree, too. He noticed she'd gone quiet again.

"What do you think?" he asked her. "If Kaley and I go there, will you come with us?"

The teenager added, "We can look at the babies behind the glass. It'll be nice to focus on people being born in a hospital instead of dying there."

Ryan realized that there was more to Kaley's suggestion than just him and Victoria. Clearly, Kaley's mom had died in a hospital. He thought about the loss his daughter had suffered and how she was still working on ways to cope with her grief. Among the three of them, emotions ran high.

He studied Victoria, waiting for a response to his question. Kaley was also looking at her.

Waiting, as well.

Chapter Three

Victoria would rather walk headfirst into a hornet's nest than visit the maternity ward with Ryan by her side. But if it would soothe Kaley's feelings about life and death, then she wasn't about to refuse.

She said, "Of course I'll go with both of you."

"Can we bring our new bears with us when we get them?" Kaley asked.

Victoria nodded, even though the stuffed animals were part of the problem. Knowing that Ryan had planned to bring her and Kaley such sweet little gifts made her miss the boy she'd once loved. And she didn't want to miss him. She'd banished him from her heart for a reason.

"Do either of you care if I tell my dad about this?" Kaley asked. "I want him to know what happened between you guys when I was born and how we're going to try to make it better."

"Tell him whatever you think is necessary." Victoria wasn't going to stand in the way, not if it gave Kaley comfort to talk to her father.

Ryan took the same approach and agreed, as well. But Victoria expected as much. Refusing would have been an injustice to their daughter.

Kaley relaxed. "Oh, good. I don't like keeping secrets from my dad. Besides, I think he's going to agree that all of us going to the hospital will be the right thing to do." The teen softly added, "My mom would have thought so, too."

The discussion ended on a sentimental note.

Ryan suggested a movie on cable, and he and Kaley checked listings and chose a comedy to lift their spirits. But watching a funny movie didn't ease Victoria's mind.

Later that night, she struggled to sleep.

She glanced at the alarm clock and wished that morning would come, because each day that passed would bring her closer to getting through this week and going home.

Finally, daylight arrived and she climbed out of bed. She opened her blinds and gazed at the country view.

After a reflective moment, she headed for the bathroom that she shared with Kaley. Her daughter's door was still closed. Ryan's door was at the other end of the hall and she could see that it was shut, as well. Assuming she was the first one up, she got ready.

Upon her bathroom departure, she noticed the other doors remained closed.

Alone in the quiet, she crept downstairs and went into the kitchen. She'd told Ryan that she would be cooking while she was here, but she wasn't going to prepare anything until he and Kaley were up. Still, it wouldn't hurt to see what type of breakfast fixings were available.

The egg keeper was full, which didn't surprise her, considering the chickens in Ryan's yard. He had fresh milk and fresh cream, too, courtesy of his cow. As she poked around in the fridge, she noticed a package of honey-cured ham and a small block of cheddar cheese. Potatoes and bread were also handy.

Needing a caffeine boost, she made a pot of coffee and sat at the old-style Formica-topped table, which looked a lot like the one Ryan and his dad used to have in their kitchen. Was it the same table? Had Ryan taken possession of it after his dad died?

And what about Ryan's wife? Had she lived here with him, or did he buy this place after they split? Victoria chastised herself for caring. His ex-wife shouldn't matter. Yet the other woman, whoever she was, crowded her already-cluttered mind.

The door from the mudroom opened, and Victoria started.

Someone entered the kitchen, and she turned around, preparing to see Ryan. The steps were too heavy to be Kaley's. Besides, what would Kaley be doing outside at this time of day? Ryan had probably been up for hours, tending to his animals, when Victoria thought he was still asleep.

Sure enough, it was him, dressed in a plain white tee, blue jeans and work boots, with his medium-length hair mussed from the morning breeze.

"The coffee smells good," he said. "I was just coming in to make a pot."

She shifted in her seat, feeling far too self-conscious,

while he stood there, looking far too gorgeous. "I beat you to it."

"That you did." He walked over to pour a cup.

She watched while he added an abundance of cream, but only one spoonful of sugar. She'd doctored hers with lots of both.

He leaned against the counter. "So Kaley isn't a morning person?"

"Sometimes she is. She was probably wiped out from yesterday."

"The traveling and everything?"

She nodded. "I'm wiped out, too."

"You don't look beat. You look pretty."

Her heart fluttered from his praise. Bad, stupid heart. "I wasn't fishing for a compliment."

"I didn't think you were. I'm just saying that the years have been good to you." He made a flat motion with his hand, mimicking the straightness of her hair. "I like the way you style your hair now. I used to like the curls, too. The way it blew every which way."

She made a face. "And frizzed up in the rain. A constant issue with the weather here."

"You were always tying scarves around your head or pulling your hoodie up real tight. My favorite times were when you'd get caught in the rain without a cover-up."

"That didn't happen very often."

"It was still fun."

He smiled, and she battled the bewitchment that was Ryan.

A few minutes later, Kaley walked into the kitchen. The product of their union, Victoria thought. She'd more or less stumbled out of bed. She was still wearing her pajamas, and on her feet were novelty slippers that looked like fuzzy creatures with eyeballs. She called them her purple people eaters after an old song she thought was funny.

"Morning," Victoria quickly said. "Now that you're here, I'll start breakfast. Ham and cheese omelets with hash browns on the side."

"Yum. Okay. Thanks." Kaley plopped down at the table and said, "Hey," to Ryan.

"Hey, yourself." He smiled at her outfit.

Victoria began by peeling potatoes. She loved cooking for her daughter, relishing the mommy feeling it gave her. She would have to be careful that whipping up meals for Ryan didn't create a wifely feeling. Old dreams. Old bewitchments. This was not a family in the making.

Ryan said to Kaley, "I got the box down from the attic this morning. So anytime you're ready, we can look through it."

"Really? Wow. That was fast."

No kidding, Victoria thought. Not only had he spent time outside, he'd rummaged around in the attic, too.

"We can look through it after breakfast," Kaley said. "Then afterward, I'll get my photo album." She grinned. "We can have a picture party."

Ryan grinned, too. Boyish as hell. Victoria cursed the knee-jerk reaction it gave her.

He said to their daughter, "Too bad we don't have any cake and ice cream to go with it."

Kaley tapped her purple people eaters together, making the eyeballs roll around. "Victoria is going to teach me to bake."

"Yes, she told me. That'll be cool. You two can fatten me up while you're here."

He was still leaning against the counter, with his lean male hips and whipcord arms. Cake and ice cream wasn't about to fatten him up. Funny thing, too, he probably stayed in shape from his country-fresh lifestyle, hiking and biking and lifting bales of hay, whereas Victoria belonged to a trendy gym, taking scheduled classes and running on a treadmill like a hamster on a wheel.

He refilled his coffee and asked Kaley, "Do you want a cup?"

"No thanks. I'm more of a cappuccino girl."

"With purple feet?" He chuckled. "There's a gourmet coffee machine in the break room at the clinic. It's one of those single-serve models with disposable brewing cups. No one ever really uses it. I can bring it in here, if that suits you."

She shot him a winning smile. "Thanks. That'd be super."

He left by way of the mudroom.

After he was gone, Kaley sad, "He's nice. He's handsome, too, for the dad type. But so is my dad. I wonder if they're going to become friends."

"They're not going to know each other very well, honey. It could be a long time before they ever meet."

"Why? Because they live so far away? They're going to have to hang out, eventually. I want both of them to be at my college graduation."

"You're only just starting school in the fall. You've got at least a full four years to go."

"I know, but there are other things, too. Like me getting married and having kids. If they don't become friends, stuff like that will be awkward for everyone."

"Let's focus on one life-altering event at a time." Victoria didn't want to consider how many times in the future that *she* would be required to see Ryan.

He returned with the gourmet coffeemaker and set it up, brewing a single cup of flavored cappuccino for Kaley.

Victoria finished making breakfast and set the table.

"This is nice," Ryan said, as the three them sat down.

Apparently Kaley thought so, too. She hummed while she ate, tucked cozily between her birth parents. Victoria was glad that her daughter was enjoying herself, but that still didn't make them a family.

Ryan remarked how good the food was, and Kaley agreed, marveling over the fact that they were feasting on fresh eggs and drinking milk provided by a miniature cow.

"This feels so fifties," Kaley said.

"That's the era this table is from," Ryan told her. "It belonged to my dad."

Victoria spoke up. "I've been wondering if it was the same one."

He shifted his attention to her. "You recognized it?"

She nodded. Everything about the past was resurfacing. Everything she'd worked so doggone hard to forget.

He said, "When I first bought this place, Dad moved in with me because he was recovering from a stroke. He insisted that he was going to get well and to move back out on his own. So I put all of his stuff in storage, including this table." He ran his fingers along the Formica. "But Dad didn't get well. About a year later, he had another stroke and died. I ended up keeping the table, maybe because it had been around for so long."

"How long?" Kaley asked.

"Since before my mom died, and I was five when it happened."

"How did she die?"

"In a car crash. I was too young to hear the specifics, and I never asked about it later. Soon after she died, Dad boxed up any reminders of her, and that was pretty much the end of it. She was a wife and mother who no longer existed."

"That's sad," Kaley said.

Victoria thought so, too. It also explained why his childhood home had been devoid of pictures or mementos.

Kaley turned quiet. Thinking, it appeared, about Ryan's family. Then she asked, "Did your dad ever date anyone after she was gone?"

"There were a few women, but nothing serious. Mostly he kept to himself."

"My dad hasn't dated, and if he has, then it hasn't gone well. He never brings anyone home. I don't think that's healthy." She turned to Victoria. "Do you?"

Victoria frowned. She rarely dated, and the boy she'd once loved was still alive—and seated right across from her, of all things. "People need time to grieve."

"It's been seven years." Kaley was frowning, too. "I want my dad to have someone in his life."

"I know, but he has to want a relationship. And contrary to popular belief, there's nothing wrong with being alone. My parents think that I should be married by now. But we all need to do what's right for us."

Victoria could feel Ryan watching her. He'd obviously never been involved in a discussion like this. But he hadn't remained alone, not the way she had. He'd

been married and divorced in the time frame that she'd
been determined to stay single.

Kaley said to her, "What if someone doesn't know
what's right for them? What if my dad doesn't know?"

Victoria replied, "You need to trust him to find his
own way. He's an amazing guy, and he's done a wonderful job raising you. When the time comes for him
to date, he'll handle it just fine."

"I hope so."

They finished eating, and Victoria cleared the table,
grateful to keep busy.

"Should I go get the stuff from the attic?" Ryan asked
Kaley.

"Definitely." The teenager sounded anxious to get
started on his side of the family tree.

He left the room and returned with a battered box.
By now, Victoria was at the sink, rinsing dishes and
getting them ready for the dishwasher.

He and Kaley sat down and began rummaging
through the contents of the box. Kaley had a spiral note-
book and pen beside her, preparing to catalog items of
interest.

Were there pictures of Ryan's ex amid the stacks of
stuff they'd dumped on the table? Or documents associated with her, such as his marriage certificate or divorce decree? Or did the box contain only things from
his childhood, the hidden-away mementos his dad had
stored?

Ryan said to Kaley, "This is my mom. It's a little
faded, but it's her."

Curiosity piqued, Victoria forgot about Ryan's ex and
focused on his mother. She dried her hands and wan-

dered over to the table and stood behind Kaley's chair.
"Can I see, too?"

He showed it to both of them.

The woman in the Polaroid appeared to be in her late
teens, probably around Kaley's age, and was dressed in
shimmery 1970s garb. Tall and thin, with long brown
hair and a natural smile, she represented the free, fun
sign of her times.

"Her maiden name was Margaret Dodd," Ryan said.
"But she went by Molly."

"She was pretty," Kaley said. "She looks happy, too."

He studied the image. "She was from the Paiute Nation, but I never met any of her family. I asked my dad
once why no one from her side ever came to see me.
He said that she'd been raised by an old aunt who'd already passed on."

"What band was your mom from?"

"I have no idea. The Paiute are divided into three
groups, with quite a number of tribes among them. I
assume she was registered with one of their federally
recognized tribes, because when I signed the adoption
papers for you, my dad said that he would provide the
documents they needed for the Indian Child Welfare
Act. At the time, I didn't think about what that meant.
But later I realized that he'd probably given them my
mom's registration papers and whatever else they required to prove what tribe I was connected to."

Kaley took Molly's picture and put it with her note-
book. "I'm going to find out more about her."

Ryan uncovered more snapshots of his mom, some
of which he and his father were in. Molly was a bit
fuller-figured than her earlier self, but just as pretty.
Victoria felt an uncomfortable tug at her heart, seeing

Ryan as a wide-eyed toddler, clinging to his dad, who was a much younger, gentler version of the man Victoria remembered.

"What was your dad's name?" Kaley asked.

"Kevin. Kevin Gregory Nash," he amended, reciting his father's full name.

As the research session continued, Victoria was compelled to stay where she was, standing beside the table, allowing herself to become immersed in Ryan's roots.

Would things have been different if his mother had lived? Would Molly have encouraged Victoria and Ryan to keep Kaley? Would she have been someone Victoria could have confided in?

Questions with dreamy answers.

Victoria wanted to believe that Molly would have been supportive, comforting her in a way that her own parents and Ryan's dad had been incapable of. She even imagined putting her head on Molly's shoulder.

"Look what I found," Kaley said.

Victoria snapped out of her daydream. Apparently Kaley had reached into the box and discovered a high school annual. Victoria inspected the cover and noticed that it was from Ryan's senior year. By then she'd already moved to California. Naturally, she was curious to see his senior photo, certain that Kaley would search for it.

As predicted, the teenager paged through the yearbook, stopping when she found her prize. "Wow. Check you out, Ryan."

"Yeah, check out how awful I look."

No, Victoria thought. He was young and handsome, just as she remembered, with his straight dark hair and exotic features, but she understood what he meant. He seemed lost in the picture, with a smile that didn't embrace his eyes.

He said, "That wasn't good a time in my life."

"Because of what happened with me," Kaley said.

He nodded.

The girl softly asked, "What did your dad say about you not going to the hospital?"

"He got raging mad. He thought it was terrible. And for once he'd been right to yell at me. By then I was used to it, though. He was always on edge about something, always bitching me out."

"I'll bet he was so grumpy all the time because he missed your mom." Kaley offered her take on the situation. "But he still should have been nicer to you. My dad has always been nice to me."

Victoria was incredibly thankful that their daughter had been adopted into a loving home. But that didn't change the past. It didn't change the ache that Ryan's senior photo caused, either.

Kaley closed the annual and said to Victoria, "You never showed me the yearbooks you were in."

"Because I don't have them anymore."

"What happened to them?"

Before Victoria could respond, Ryan interjected. "She probably got rid of them on purpose."

Victoria sighed. "You're right, I did. I tossed out everything associated with that era. It was easier to start over, especially after I moved."

He made the same admission. "I didn't keep the yearbooks you were in, either. That's the only one I still have."

Kaley shook her head. "You guys were so dramatic,

throwing things out. But you're both kind of sweet, too, in your own weird way."

Ryan laughed a little, maybe because he didn't know what else to do. Then he said to Victoria, "I always thought you were sweet."

She shrugged, trying to appear unaffected by their emotional weirdness. "What can I say? I was a nice girl."

"And you smelled really good."

"That's not the same kind of sweet."

"I know, but you always smelled like dessert or something."

Because she used to douse herself in vanilla-scented lotion. "I wore too much fragrance."

"Not to me."

Instantly, she was reminded of him burying his nose in her sugary skin. Oh, the memories that evoked: curling up in Ryan's bed when his dad wasn't home, slipping her greedy hands into his half-undone clothes, closing her eyes while he peeled hers off. Even now, her eyes were starting to drift closed, until she realized that Ryan was looking at her.

She told herself to get a grip. But it didn't work. She couldn't get her memories under control. "I think I should go now."

He made a puzzled expression. "Go?"

"To my room. To get some work done." She needed to escape. If she didn't, those intimate feelings would only get stronger. "You two have fun with the rest of the family tree."

"Okay. See you later." Kaley handled her impeding departure with ease. But she'd already shifted her attention back to the box, unaware of Victoria's discomfort.

Ryan noticed, though. She could feel him watching her.

She walked away, praying for the strength to make it through the rest of the week without feeling more for him than she should.

Ryan and Kaley stayed in the kitchen and finished going through everything.

Afterward, she said, "I'm going to go get my photo album now."

"Sounds good." He was eager to continue spending time with her. But he was disappointed that Victoria had left. It had been nice to have her nearby. But she was skittish around him. One little smell-good remark and she'd made a mad dash for the doorway.

Kaley left to get her photo album, and he stood up to stretch his legs.

She returned, and they resumed their seats. He braced himself for the newborn pictures of her, which he assumed would be on the first page.

He assumed right. As he gazed at the images and studied her cap of dark hair and scrunched-up little face, he wanted to zap back in time and hold her as close as he possibly could.

"You were beautiful," he said. He imagined that she would have felt small and soft in his arms.

"I think I look kind of goofy."

"No. You were beautiful. Absolutely perfect." He lifted his gaze. "You still are."

"Thanks." She got a little shy, ducking her head.

He realized that without Victoria in the room with them, they didn't know quite how to behave. He and his daughter were strangers.

She turned the next page. "This is me and my mom and dad. I think I was about three months old here."

Her parents were an attractive couple: the mom was a summer blonde and the dad was tall and dark. Ryan envied the happy looks on their faces. But then he reminded himself that the mother was gone and the father was alone and missing her.

He said, "Victoria told me that your mom's name was Corrine and that she was adopted, too."

Kaley nodded. "She never knew her birth parents and always felt as if something was missing from her life."

"Did she ever try to find them?"

"Yes, but nothing ever surfaced. She was really upset later when she discovered that she couldn't have kids. She wanted a baby of her own more than anything. But then she decided that not being able to conceive meant that she was destined to adopt."

Ryan glanced at the picture of Corrine and Eric, imagining them in his mind: their love for each other, their determination to become parents.

Kaley said, "When they first started the adoption proceedings, they were only interested in open adoptions. Because of the way my mom felt about her childhood, they wanted the birth mother to be involved in their baby's life. The birth father, too, if he was around. Lots of times the dads aren't."

That struck a guilty chord. In the end, Ryan had been one of those dads.

Kaley continued, "After a couple of years, they were still waiting for a newborn. But they were warned that it might take a while. Then finally the adoption agency called and told them that there was a baby coming up who was part Native and had to go to a Native home, which would put them at the top of the list since my dad is registered with the Cherokee Nation. But they had to agree to a closed adoption or not take the baby."

"So they agreed," he said, stating the obvious.

"Yep. Later, when I was old enough to understand, Mom said that if I ever wanted to search for my birth family or learn more about my roots, she would help me."

"But that never interested you until now?"

"I didn't see the point. I had great parents. What did I need another family for? Even after Mom died, I didn't think it mattered."

"Then what changed for you? Why did you search for Victoria and me?"

"Everything seemed different after I turned eighteen. Maybe it's the being-an-adult thing and getting ready for college. It's like I'm someone new. Only sometimes I'm not sure who that person is." She wrinkled her forehead. "Does that sound dumb?"

"Not at all. Sometimes I'm not sure who I am, either." The son of deceased parents, an ex-husband, Victoria's former boyfriend, Kaley's confused birth father. None of his titles sounded sure or steady. "The easiest way for me to define myself is through my work." That part of his life was sure and steady.

"Your work seems noble. Taking care of animals."

"It makes me happy." So did her describing his life's passion as noble. "Victoria told me that you're going to major in business with a minor in women's studies. Why did you choose women's studies as your minor? What drew you to it?"

"I think women need to be empowered, and this is my way of being part of that movement. And with me being from two cultures, I think my perspective is especially important."

Suddenly she seemed so mature, so strong, a warrior in the making. "Have you considered what type of job you're going to pursue?"

"Not yet. With the way the world is now, who knows where it will lead me? It's scary that an education doesn't guarantee you a job now."

"I have a feeling you'll do just fine."

"Thanks." She smiled at him.

He smiled, too, and they returned to the photo album.

The next few pages consisted of pictures taken after her mother was gone. Ryan could tell because Kaley was older in them.

She said, "I added these. Mom started the album, and I kept it going."

He noticed how telling those images were, the obvious closeness between Eric and Kaley after they'd lost Corrine.

He thought about what Victoria had said about Eric, how good and kind and amazing he was. He also thought about how badly Kaley wanted her father to start dating and move on with his life.

Would Victoria ever consider dating Eric? Would their friendship eventually move in that direction? It actually seemed logical and possible, too. They lived near each other and probably had common interests.

Ryan couldn't imagine Eric not wanting Victoria. What man wouldn't be attracted to her, especially the man who'd raised the child Victoria had birthed? Talk about a bond.

He turned the page and saw what appeared to be a

recent picture of Eric. Ryan was having a bit of trouble liking the guy, with envy rearing its ugly head.

The next picture was of Eric, Kaley and Victoria, smiling together like a family. His stomach turned tight.

He glanced up at his daughter. "Do you want to go to the store today and get those teddy bears?" He desperately needed to bond with her. And Victoria, too. He wanted them to seem like a family. He wanted the same advantage as Eric.

"Sure. I'd love that."

"Maybe we can take some pictures to include in your album of the three of us. You, me and Victoria."

"That's a great idea. I'll go tell her." She hopped out of her chair. "This is going to be fun."

He doubted that Victoria was going to feel the same sense of elation. But he wasn't giving up on her this week. He was going to win her over, the best he could.

Chapter Four

On the way to the store, Victoria rode shotgun in Ryan's truck, and Kaley sat in the extended cab backseat, immersed in her smartphone. Victoria would have preferred to be in back. Sitting next to Ryan made her feel like his partner or his girlfriend or something that identified her with him. It also made her think about his ex-wife. Not knowing anything about the other woman was driving her crazy. But asking him would be worse. It would prove that she cared, and she didn't want to care.

Ryan glanced in the rearview mirror and said to Kaley, "Are you texting?"

"No. Twittering," came the reply. "About us."

"Us?" He sounded pleased.

"You, me and Victoria. I'm letting my followers know that I'm hanging out with both of my birth parents this week."

He smiled. "That's cool." He looked at Victoria. "She's Twittering about us."

"That's what they do these days." She didn't mind being the subject of her daughter's tweets, except that she was being linked with Ryan.

"Do you Twitter?" he asked her.

"Yes. But not personal things. I use my account for business."

"Maybe I should open an account." He shot another glance in the mirror. "I could follow you, Kaley."

"That would be great," the teen said.

Nothing about this was great, Victoria thought. Except that it was making Kaley happy, she amended. That was extremely important. That was the whole point.

They arrived at their destination and went inside.

As they headed for the toy department, Victoria imagined Ryan coming here when he'd bought the original bears. Had he been nervous, trying to decide what to choose?

Even now, he seemed a little nervous, as if he were remembering the moment. But there was a light in his eyes, too, that sparkled for Kaley. The teenager walked ahead of them, her long hair swishing.

"I'm so glad we're doing this," Ryan said to Victoria.

"I know you are. Kaley is, too."

"But you're not."

"I'm trying." She spoke quietly so their daughter couldn't hear what they were saying.

"It's been a long time coming. Something I never even dreamed would happen. You, me and our little girl."

"For a week," she reminded him. Not forever.

"A wonderful week."

Wonderful for him and Kaley. Victoria had butter-flies flapping around in her stomach. Butterflies? They were more like bats.

Kaley found the stuffed animal aisle and motioned, full-steam ahead. "This way."

Her parents followed.

Once they were surrounded by fuzzy creatures, Kaley asked Ryan, "What did the first ones look like?"

"They were brown with pink ribbons around their necks. And they were about this size." He picked up a small giraffe to demonstrate. "But they were really soft. The plush kind."

Kaley walked up and down the aisle, looking for something similar to what he'd described. Ryan helped her, obviously relying on his memory. Victoria didn't participate. She merely waited, letting them to choose whatever felt right to them.

The stuffed toys were grouped by brand, not type, making the search more intense. Dogs, cats, monkeys, elephants, penguins, leopards, pretty much everything that could be fashioned into a furry critter lined the shelves.

Finally, Ryan located what they were looking for. "There." He reached up and removed two smiling teddy bears.

Kaley snagged one of them from him. "Oh, look how cute they are." She made her bear dance. "Only they aren't wearing ribbons."

Ryan said, "I know. But other than that, they're al-most the same."

Kaley had a solution. "We can go to the notions de-partment and get some pink ribbon."

That was what the three of them did, with Kaley carrying her bear and Ryan carrying the one that would become Victoria's.

After two pieces of ribbon were measured and cut from a spool, they waited in a checkout lane. Ryan paid for everything with his ATM card.

Inside the truck, he and Kaley fitted the bears with their new collars, tying them into pretty bows.

It was then that he turned Victoria's gift over to her.

She thanked him and placed it on her lap, trying to remain detached.

"We should name them," Kaley said. "How about Pinky and Poppy?"

"After your nail polish?" Victoria knew she favored a color called pink poppy.

"Yep." The nail polish wearer waggled her fingers at Ryan. "See?"

"That's nice." He remained behind the wheel, without buckling his seat belt or starting the engine. "But don't let Perky and Pesky get a hold of Pinky and Poppy."

Kaley laughed at the obvious tongue twister. "We won't." She said to Victoria, "Yours can be Pinky, okay?"

"Okay." Without thinking, she patted its fluffy head. Now that it had been christened, she couldn't help but treat it as if it were real.

Kaley made Poppy peer over Victoria's shoulder. "Where are you going to keep her?"

"What do you mean?"

"When you get home. Where are to going to put Pinky?"

"I don't know." She was only just getting used to the bear.

"Poppy is going to sleep on my bed."

"Do you have other stuffed toys on your bed?" Ryan asked.

"Not anymore. I did when I was younger. But Poppy is different. She's part of the grown-up me."

Victoria thought that the toy was bringing out the child in Kaley, making her seem more like a kid than an adult. But she'd lost a portion of her childhood when her mother had died, and if this was helping her regain it, even unknowingly, then she had every right to bask in the feeling.

Kaley reclined in her seat. "As long as we're out and we have Pinky and Poppy with us, we should go to the hospital."

Oh, God, Victoria thought. That dreaded place, those ghostly halls. She didn't want to go there, not today, not tomorrow, not any time this week, but she'd promised that she would. And with the bears being so fresh and sweet and making her daughter so happy, how could she put a damper on it?

Hiding her emotions, she said, "That's up to Ryan. He's the driver."

He replied, "For sure. Let's do it."

He was as eager as Kaley. But why wouldn't he be? He was interested in making new memories, whereas Victoria just wanted to keep the old ones buried.

Off they went to the hospital.

It didn't take long to get there, and the tall gray building with its concrete walkway and manicured shrubs looked the same.

"Nothing has changed," Victoria said. "Not that I can tell."

Ryan gestured. "That's a new diner across the street."

Victoria glanced in the direction of the restaurant. It didn't count, at least not to her. "What used to be there?"

"I don't know. I can't remember."

More proof that it didn't count. The hospital itself was what mattered, the time warp that she couldn't escape.

"What floor is the maternity ward on?" Kaley asked.

"The third," Victoria responded. "Unless they moved it to another floor." Which seemed doubtful.

As Ryan searched for a parking space, Kaley asked him, "Did your dad die here?"

"No. He passed away at home."

"Was he alone?"

"I was there, and I called 911, but he died before the paramedics arrived."

"Was he in pain?"

"I don't think so. They say that when someone loses consciousness the way he did, they don't feel anything."

"That's good. My mom was in a lot of pain when she passed," Kaley said.

"I'm sorry," he said softly. Victoria was sorry, too. She knew how much Kaley had loved Corrine and how much she missed her.

"It was uterine cancer," Kaley told Ryan.

"I'm sorry," he said again. "I wish she would have survived."

Victoria wrapped her arms around Pinky and said a prayer for Corrine. She also said one for Kaley, who'd gone quiet and was probably thinking about her mother. Victoria had never dealt with the death of a loved one. Ryan had, of course. He'd lost both of his parents. She whispered a prayer for him and his family, too.

He finally nabbed a parking space, and they piled

out of his truck and entered the building, taking the bears with them.

Victoria checked the directory. The maternity ward was still on the third floor. They took the elevator.

Kaley glanced over at her. "Do you remember which room you stayed in?"

That wasn't something she would ever forget. "Three twenty-two."

"Was there another patient with you?"

"No. They kept me separate from the other mothers since I was giving up my baby."

Kaley said, "Before we go to the nursery, can we stand beside the door to that room?"

With her heart thumping, Victoria led the way. They passed the nurses' station, their collective footsteps sounding on the sterile floor.

Room 322 was in the middle of the hallway.

"So this is it." Ryan spoke reverently to their daughter. "The place where I would have held you."

"And here we are now," the teen replied.

He nodded. "Life is full of surprises." He leaned closer to Victoria and whispered, "Thanks for doing this."

She almost reached for his hand, but she curled her fingers inward instead, fighting the temptation to touch him.

Silence streamed between them. Kaley wasn't talking, either. She seemed just as reflective as they were. But the teen seemed to know enough not to linger for too long.

She said, "I think we should check out the babies now."

"I'm not sure what direction it is." Victoria hadn't

gone anywhere near the nursery after they'd taken her newborn away.

They inquired at the nurse's station. The nurse who assisted them was too young to have been here eighteen years ago, but Victoria couldn't help but wonder if her obstetrician was still around or if he'd retired by now.

Before they headed to the nursery, she asked the nurse, "Is Dr. Jason Devlin still on staff here?"

"Not that I'm aware of. I've never heard that name."

"I was just curious. He worked here a long time ago."

As they walked away, Kaley asked, "Was that the doctor who delivered me?"

"Yes. He was especially kind to me." He'd treated her with care from the very beginning. "I really liked him."

Kaley got out her phone and ran a Google search on his name. Within minutes, she discovered that he'd passed away nearly ten years ago.

More death, Victoria thought sadly. The news made Kaley solemn until they arrived at the nursery.

"This is so cool," the teen said, as they stood on the other side of the glass. "It looks just like it does in the movies."

Victoria gazed at the newborns. Only two were present, snug as little bugs inside Plexiglas bassinets with identification cards displaying their surnames. "The rest of them are probably with their mothers. Most people keep their newborns in their rooms."

"It's still cool," Kaley commented.

Ryan moved closer, entranced, as well.

Victoria didn't know long they stood there, gazing at other people's children while in the company of the daughter they'd lost and gained, but they allowed Kaley to decide when it was time to leave.

On the way out, Victoria commended herself for surviving the dreaded hospital. Then someone called Ryan's name.

They turned around and saw a woman in a colorful uniform walking toward them. She seemed distantly familiar with her shiny brown hair and big round eyes.

"Why do I think I know her?" she asked Ryan.

"Because you do. It's Sandy from high school."

Sandy Simmons. Of all people to run into, she was one of the safest. She hadn't talked trash about Victoria or made cutting remarks about her pregnant belly like some of the other girls.

As she approached them, Victoria noticed that Sandy's name tag read Sandy McGuire, not Sandy Simmons. She was married now, obviously. In addition to her name change, she was wearing a wedding band.

Sandy said to Ryan, "I keep seeing you everywhere. Last week I brought that rascal cat of mine to your clinic, and now you're here." She smiled at Victoria and Kaley, but she didn't look at Victoria with recognition.

Ryan broke the ice with a bang. "Sandy, you remember Victoria Allen, don't you? She's visiting me this week, and she brought our daughter, Kaley, with her."

The other woman blinked her owlish eyes. "Yes, of course. Victoria. It's so good to see you." She turned toward Kaley. "And it's very nice to meet you." Sandy blinked again, caught in confusion.

It seemed apparent what she was thinking. Had Victoria changed her mind about giving up the baby and gone off to California to raise her instead?

Victoria clarified, "Kaley and I found each other on an adoption registry site, and then we contacted Ryan so he could meet Kaley, too."

Their daughter spoke up. "This is only our second day in Oregon." She waved Poppy as she spoke. "I wanted to see the hospital where I was born."

Sandy visibly relaxed. "That's wonderful. I'm happy for all of you." She tapped her name tag. "I'm a radiologist here." She said to Victoria, "I married Joe McGuire. He was from our class. Do you remember him? Oh, wait. He was new during our senior year, and by that time, you'd already left. You know what would be fun? For the three of you to come to our barbecue tomorrow. I realize it's short notice, but if you haven't made other plans, it would be wonderful to have you there. We always have these big summer bashes with our neighbors. Ryan, I'm sure there will be other clients of yours there." To Victoria, she said, "He isn't the only vet in these parts, but he's always been my favorite." She shot Victoria a look, as if she was supposed to know who the other veterinarians were. Sandy kept talking, to Kaley this time. "You'd enjoy the barbecue, too. I can introduce you to my niece. She's about your age. She's going off to some fancy college in the fall."

"Really?" Kaley sounded interested. "I'd like to meet her, and we haven't made any plans for tomorrow." She turned to Ryan. "Have we?"

He replied, "If you want to go to the barbecue then that's our plan."

Sandy clapped her hands. She'd always been the chipper type. "Oh, and I can't wait." She motioned to Victoria and Ryan. "It's nice to see you two back together."

"We're n-not..." Victoria stammered.

"...back together." Ryan finished the sentence for her. The other woman quickly clarified. "I just meant in the same town and with your daughter. Not together *together*."

The next few seconds produced an awkward lull.

Sandy stepped it up. "I better get back to work. My break is almost over. Ryan, no doubt you have my phone number and address in your office records, but I'll make it easier for you." She reached into her pocket for a business card and a pen and jotted down the information. "The barbecue is at two. It's a potluck, but you don't have to bring anything unless you want to." She said goodbye and darted off with her usual smile.

The air in Victoria's lungs whooshed out. "Sandy always was a whirlwind." And the barbecue was less than twenty-four hours away. Things were happening fast. "I think we should bring something for the potluck."

Kaley had a suggestion. "How about dessert? You were already going to teach me to bake, and this will give us an excuse to make something really cool."

Victoria agreed it was a good idea.

Ryan said, "So our next stop should be the market to get baking supplies?"

"And regular food. We can't live on sweets alone." If she was going to continue to do the cooking, then she needed to stock his kitchen.

Kaley smiled. "What a great day this is turning out to be."

It wasn't half-bad, Victoria thought. But that didn't mean that she'd changed her mind about getting close to Ryan.

She was still anxious for the week to end so she could go home.

* * *

Ryan thrived on the activity in his kitchen. This was fast becoming the favorite room in his house.

After they returned from the market and unpacked the groceries, the women got started on the baking. They decided to make cupcakes. Kaley even wanted to take the lesson a step further and decorate them in creative ways. While at the market, she'd asked Victoria if they could make them to look like cats and dogs.

"Because Ryan is the favorite vet around here," Kaley had said.

He couldn't have been prouder. But he also suspected that Victoria was wondering why Sandy had made an issue out of him not being the only vet in town. He'd seen the look Sandy had shot Victoria. He wondered if he should explain, especially since she and Kaley were making cat and dog cupcakes in his honor.

Would it ruin the moment? Or was it better to say something before it came up again? He wouldn't want Victoria or Kaley to think that he was keeping secrets from them, and it wasn't *that* big of a deal.

Well, actually, it was sort of a major deal, major in his life, anyway.

He didn't say anything, at least not yet. Otherwise he would have to interrupt the lesson, and he didn't want to take that away from Kaley.

"Don't they smell good?" his daughter said when the cupcakes were cooling on the counter.

He nodded. "It smells like a bakery." Sugary and sweet, like the fragrance Victoria used to wear.

Kaley said, "Our house used to smell like this at Christmastime. My mom was always baking. How long before we can ice them?" she asked Victoria.

"Soon," her birth mother replied.

The frosting was already made and Kaley had already tasted it, licking the beaters on the hand mixer. Ryan suspected it was a habit from her childhood and something Corrine had allowed her to do.

She sat at the table and sorted through the ingredients they would be using to create the animals' faces. She glanced up at Ryan. "Are you going to help us decorate them?"

"I can try. But they might not come out that great. I've never been the artsy type." He looked over at Victoria. "You always were." Sometimes she used to bring her sketch pad with her when they explored the woods. She was always finding something interesting to draw. She could even draw things from her imagination, such as wood nymphs and fairies and scary little trolls.

Victoria said, "Eric is an art teacher at a middle school."

Ryan started. "He is?"

"Yes, and Corrine was a youth counselor."

He glanced at Kaley. Her mom being a counselor seemed to fit. In a sense, Corrine was still guiding her daughter. Today was evidence of her influence: the hospital, the baking lesson.

Victoria said, "Eric does freelance graphic design on the side. We've been talking about doing some jobs together."

Ryan struggled not to frown. Were Eric and Victoria on their way to becoming a couple? The possibility still made him uneasy. Especially since Ryan and his ex used to work together.

Victoria said to Kaley, "We can finish the cupcakes now."

Ryan watched as they iced each mini cake. Then the decorating began. Kaley did the first one. She made a dog's face using chocolate chips for the nose and eyes, a tiny gumdrop for the mouth and cookies for the ears. It was as cute as could be and simple enough for Ryan to replicate. Victoria's designs were much more complex, like something a pastry chef would make. Soon Kaley's designs got more detailed, too, proving that she, too, had art skills. Ryan stuck with the simple versions. But overall, they worked well as a team.

Finally, he decided to mention what had been on his mind earlier. And because he didn't know how to segue into it, he more or less just blurted it out. "My ex-wife is a vet, too."

Both women looked up, but Victoria's reaction was stronger. She paused in midkitty. The cupcake she was decorating was in the form of frilly pink cat. "So that's who Sandy was talking about?"

"Yes."

"Is she from around here?"

He shook his head. "She's originally from Seattle. I met her at Washington State University. That's where we both went to school. After we graduated, we got married and decided to set up shop here. The old vet in town was retiring and offered to sell us his practice. It was an easy transition."

The pink cat was still half-done. "You had a clinic together?"

He nodded. "After the divorce, she kept that practice, and I bought this house and started a new one."

Kaley asked, "Are you still friends?"

"We're not friends, per se. But we're cordial when we see each other at chamber of commerce meetings and

Chapter Five

Victoria's curiosity heightened. She'd been wondering about Ryan's ex, and now that he'd cautiously broached the subject, it only made her more interested. But of course, she didn't want to be interested in Ryan, particularly when it concerned the woman he'd married.

Was he hurt that his ex had moved on? That she was engaged to someone else? Was he still in love with her? Had he tried to make the marriage work?

The questions in Victoria's mind were endless. She glanced over at Kaley, who was happily engrossed in the cupcakes again. She didn't seem concerned about Ryan's ex. But it was different for Victoria.

Because she'd wanted to be Ryan's wife.

God, she hated those memories, those feelings. Now she wished that she could bail out on the barbecue, but she couldn't do that to Kaley. Thing was, people would probably assume that she and Ryan were a couple. Or at least wonder about them, since Kaley would be introduced as their daughter. Sandy had said that some of Ryan's other clients would probably be there. Surely, most of his clients knew that he was divorced, especially if they'd followed him to his new practice. So wouldn't that make them curious when he showed up with Victoria and their grown daughter in tow?

Luckily, Sandy hadn't said anything about anyone else from their old high school attending the barbecue. Victoria didn't want to run into more people from the past. Dealing with the present was difficult enough.

Kaley said, "I'm going to make a cupcake that looks like Pesky." She grinned at the bulldog, who was curled up in a corner of the kitchen. "I'll make one that looks like Perky, too." Her next grin was at the border collie, also napping in the same corner.

Ryan smiled. "They'll be flattered, I'm sure."

Victoria didn't feel like smiling, but she faked it. She didn't want Kaley to know how troubled she was. "They'd probably rather eat them."

"True," Ryan said. "But they're not getting any sweets."

Kaley said to Victoria, "Will you make some that look like the bougainvillea babies?"

"Sure." Both of the flower-cats were tabbies. "I'll do them now." Trying to keep her mind occupied, she delved into the task. Not only did she make tabby faces, she added frosted bougainvilleas to the design.

"Oh, wow." Kaley praised the end result. "Those are great. I'm going take pictures of the cupcakes so I can email them to my dad. He's going to love the ones of our cats." She got her camera and snapped some close-ups.

Afterward, she said, "We need to take pictures of ourselves with Poppy and Pinky, too, for the photo album."

A short time later, the teddy bear session began. Ryan was the cameraman for those, holding it at arm's length so he could capture everyone, including the toys, which Victoria and Kaley were holding. The teenager stood in the middle, mugging it up.

Always ready for more action, Kaley said, "Let's do some separate shots, too. Me alone with each of you."

Victoria preferred those. Keeping things "separate" was much more comfortable.

Just when she thought it was over, Kaley had another idea. "Let me take some of you guys together."

Her and Ryan? By themselves? Victoria wanted to refuse, but it was better to go with the flow than make an obvious fuss. Still, when Ryan moved next to her, her heart pounded something fierce. He was way too close. He even reached across to put his arm around her.

Tactile sensations.

The warmth of his body. The flutter that being near him used to stir. It wasn't fair that she was experiencing that same type of flutter again.

She was astute enough to know that Ryan was feeling the attraction, too. The energy between them was as thick as the vines that grew in the woods. As tangled, too. Victoria could barely breathe.

Kaley took several pictures of them, and it was the longest snap-snap of Victoria's life. Finally Ryan dropped his arm and stepped away from her. She avoided his gaze. He seemed to be avoiding hers, as well. Thankfully Kaley didn't seem to notice the tension in the air. She was too busy checking out the digital images.

"I'm going to go to my room and email the cupcake pictures to Dad now," she said. "I should send some of the teddy bear ones, too, so he can see all of us together. And I should probably call him. He's always happy when I do."

She darted off with an exuberant swoosh, leaving Victoria and Ryan alone, their attraction looming.

Silence.

Victoria realized that she was still holding Pinky, hugging the bear to her breast. She set it down.

More silence.

He glanced at the treats they'd made. For a diversion, maybe?

Then he said, "Is it okay if I eat a cupcake? Maybe one of the cookie-eared dogs since they aren't as fancy as the others?"

He was having a sugar craving? Now? It made her think of the vanilla lotion she used to wear. The sweetness he favored. Was that part of his craving?

She blew out a breath. "Of course you can have one. Any one you want."

He stuck with one of his non-fancy creations. He broke a piece of it off and put it in his mouth. She tried not to watch. But she failed, miserably. She was staring at him. Damn. She blinked, turned away.

He said, "Do you want a bite?"

Double damn. She turned back to him. "No, thank you."

"Are you sure? It's really good."

"I'm positive." She imagined him feeding it to her... like wedding cake. She frowned and thought about his former wife. Did he have a big traditional wedding? A romantic honeymoon? Did his gut wrench whenever he saw his ex with her new man?

"What's wrong?"

"Nothing." She couldn't tell him how much it hurt that he'd married someone else, not without letting her guard down.

Maybe tomorrow she would ask Sandy about Ryan's ex and hopefully get answers to her questions.

Without ever having to discuss it with him.

The following day, they headed to the barbecue and discovered that Sandy's house was located in Victoria's old neighborhood.

Ryan glanced over at her. "Blast from the past."

Victoria nodded. "This town is full of them." She couldn't flee from the discomfort it caused, no matter how hard she tried.

"What are you guys talking about?" Kaley asked from the backseat.

Victoria replied, "I grew up around here."

Kaley bobbed her head, as if she was trying to see past Ryan's shoulder. "Where?"

"A few streets over."

"Can we go see your house?"

She didn't want to make a stubborn fuss, but she didn't want to encourage her daughter, either. "There's nothing special about it. It's just typical suburbia, like the rest of the houses in this track." Ticky-tacky homes built in the era in which Victoria had been born, with mature landscape and tidy sidewalks. "Little colored boxes, as they say."

"Are you kidding? It's where you used to live. That's epic, especially since you lived there with me in your belly." Kaley kept bobbing. "That makes it my old house, too."

Victoria looked over at Ryan, and he smiled. Apparently Kaley's comment had amused him. It was sweet, Victoria thought. She gestured for him to take them there.

He knew the way, of course.

Soon he pulled up to a blue-and-white house and kept the motor running. "I haven't been back here since you left, Victoria. God, it seems weird."

For her, too. She'd never expected to return. "It has a new fence." She gestured. "That planter is new, too."

"Which room was yours?" Kaley asked.

"You can't see it. It's in the back," Victoria told her.

Ryan said, "I couldn't throw pebbles at her window. I always wanted to, though. I always thought that seemed romantic."

Kaley laughed. "Seriously? No one does that."

"I'll bet people do."

"Yeah, on TV and in the movies."

Victoria rolled her eyes. They were acting like a couple of kids, arguing about foolishness. "You're both being silly."

"Admit it," Ryan said to her. "You would have liked it if I'd shown up in the middle of the night at your window."

"Like a vampire? I don't think so."

"Ooh." Kaley made a swooning motion. "I think vampires are sexy."

"See?" Ryan went smug.

"Gross." The teenager made a face at him. "I wasn't saying that you were sexy."

"I know, smarty. But Victoria thought I was. I was the hot ticket in my day."

Kaley made another face. "Now I'm really grossed out."

Victoria kept quiet. Ryan had been just about every girl's dream in high school, including hers.

"I really was—"

Before he could finish, Kaley play-smacked the back of his head. "Let's go to the barbecue before you bore us to death with your tales of conceit."

He chuckled. Then he pulled away from the curb and went serious. He said to Victoria, "One thing no one can deny is that your parents never liked me. They were never keen on us dating."

They'd disliked him even more after he'd gotten her into trouble. She glanced back at Kaley. But that "trouble" had turned out to be best thing that ever happened to Victoria. "My parents' opinions don't matter."

"Then why are you so sensitive about how they react to everything?"

Kaley complained. "You guys are going to ruin a perfectly good day if you keep talking about this kind of stuff."

"Sorry." Ryan quickly apologized.

"So am I." Victoria added her apology. But it was for more than the downer conversation. She was apologizing for giving Kaley up when she'd desperately wanted to keep her.

But if she had kept her, what type of life would Kaley have had, with Victoria being so young and her parents being so unsupportive?

She frowned, staring out the windshield. It was confusing to feel this way, to keep analyzing the past, to be so mixed-up.

They arrived at Sandy's house, and she put on a happy face.

But it didn't help. Hours later, she was still mixed-up.

The barbecue itself was festive with a slew of yummy food: chips, dips and side dishes galore. The main course, provided by Sandy and her husband, Joe, ranged from hot dogs and hamburgers to shish kebabs. Although the buffet tables were filled with desserts, the cupcakes were a noticeable hit. Most of the other guests were couples with small children, which was part of why the cupcakes went over so well. Even Joe and Sandy had little kids.

Victoria's predictions about how she and Ryan would be perceived were spot-on. Those who knew him seemed curious, and those who'd never met him before automatically assumed that he and Victoria were married. Both she and Ryan hastily explained the "adoption reunion" to the people who made the wrong assumption.

At one point, Sandy leaned over and quietly said to her, "I didn't tell people ahead of time about you because to me that would have seemed like gossip, and you dealt with enough of that back in high school."

Naturally, Victoria wanted to question Sandy about Ryan's ex, but the opportunity hadn't presented itself for a private discussion.

Kaley and Sandy's niece, a bright-eyed blonde named June, befriended each other right away. So much so, Victoria suspected that Kaley had just made a friend for life. They appeared to have a lot in common, including their zest for women's rights. As Victoria watched them, she marveled at Kaley's ever-changing nature.

Yesterday she'd seemed young and girlish, making pet-inspired cupcakes and posing for teddy bear pictures, and today she was behaving with maturity and grace. Had Victoria been like that at her age, too? At the moment, she hardly knew who she was, then or now.

As for Ryan, he was sitting at a table with a group of men discussing an upcoming poker game to which he'd been invited. As far as she could tell, he hadn't agreed to attend the gambling event. But he talked and laughed easily with the rest of the guys. Still, every so often, he looked at her in the same bewildered way that she was looking at him. Was it because people had mistakenly referred to her as his wife?

She understood why Sandy hadn't told anyone ahead of time. There were at least forty people in attendance. Singling Ryan and Victoria out would have been odd. Sandy had done the right thing by letting them handle it themselves.

But were they handling it?

Thank goodness Kaley was having a spectacular time. By now, she and June were conversing with some of the younger children.

As the barbecue wore down, Sandy showed Victoria her vegetable garden. It was then, amid rows of carrots, beets and tomatoes, that she forged ahead with the topic that had been burning inside her brain.

"How well do you know Ryan's ex-wife?"

"Not well," Sandy replied. "I used to see her from time to time at their old clinic. But Ryan has always been our primary vet, so he was the one who treated our cats. I never said much to Jackie except polite pleasantries."

Jackie? At least now Victoria knew her name. "Ryan

mentioned that they met in college and came back here afterward to start their practice. And that she's engaged to someone else now."

"Is that all he told you about her?"

"Pretty much." She paused. "So what's she like? What do you think of her?"

"She seemed okay to me when they were married, a little on the quiet side, but nice enough. After they broke up, though, I started wondering about her."

"What do you mean?"

"Because of how quickly she and Don Compton got together." Sandy made tight expression. "Maybe a bit too soon?"

"You think she was cheating on Ryan with him?"

"I don't know. It just seemed strange that she and Don hooked up so soon. But maybe it's just me being protective of Ryan. I always wanted him to marry you. Silly, I know, since you two were just kids."

Victoria couldn't bear to admit that she'd wanted the same thing then.

Sandy said, "I could tell that you were struggling with the idea of giving up the baby. You seemed so lost, cradling your big belly when you thought no one was looking."

Her heart ached with the memory, with a fragile image of herself as a pregnant teen, trying to calm the baby kicking inside her and feeling as if she was wearing a scarlet letter. "Apparently you saw the real me."

"I've always been a people watcher. I try not to be a busybody, though. You don't think I am, do you?"

"Not at all." She thought Sandy was kind and gently observant. "I appreciate your talking to me about this."

"I'm sorry I couldn't shed much light on Jackie for

you. I guess if you want to know more about what happened between her and Ryan, you'll have to ask him."

Yes, Victoria, thought. Eventually, she would. Either that or forget about it altogether, and somehow she didn't see that happening.

Not when her curiosity had already come this far.

On the drive back to the farmhouse, Ryan assessed the barbecue. In spite of the adoption explanation, people had treated him, Victoria and Kaley like a family, and he'd appreciated the association, at least where Kaley had been concerned. With Victoria, it had been awkward, as usual. But they'd gotten through it and now they were home.

They went inside and the canines greeted them, with Pesky dancing around Kaley's feet. "Everyone loved our cupcakes," she told the bulldog. "A boy named Kirk ate the one that looked like you." She addressed Perky. "A little girl named Whitney ate yours. But she felt bad about biting into your face. I told her it was okay. That you'd want her to."

Ryan couldn't stop from smiling. "Victoria used to feel bad about eating those marshmallow Peeps at Easter."

She waved away his comment. "I did not."

"Yes, you did. You'd always say 'poor birdie' before you gobbled it up."

"I was just goofing around."

"I know. But it always made me laugh. I gave you a big basket of Easter goodies the second year we were together. Do you remember that?"

"Yes. Peeps in every color. Tons of jelly beans, too.

But you removed all of the licorice ones before you dumped them in there."

"Because you said that you didn't like them."

She wrinkled her nose. "I still don't."

"Sounds like you were a nice boyfriend," Kaley said, as she plopped onto the sofa.

He made a bad joke. "Except for the part about not showing up at the hospital? Yeah, I was the best."

His daughter actually laughed. "Picking out the jelly beans doesn't make up for that."

"Gee, and I was hoping it did."

Victoria shook her head. "You two aren't funny."

"No, but apparently we have the same twisted sense of humor." He sat next to Kaley and nudged her shoulder, trying to seem like a dad. "Me and my kid."

She nudged him back, making him feel like a million bucks. Then she said, "Would it be all right if I hung out with June tomorrow? We had a lot of fun together, and I'd really like to see her again before I have to go home."

The million bucks feeling went flat. Ryan was glad that she'd made a new friend, but already the week was racing by, with only four more days left, and she wanted to use up one of those days with someone else. What could he say? That he didn't want her to spend time with one of her peers? That he wanted her to himself?

He replied, "Of course you can hang out with June."

"Okay. Thanks. She invited me to go to her house. Then we were thinking of seeing a movie."

"Sounds like you have a full day planned."

"Yeah. Her boyfriend just broke up with her because he's jealous that she's going away to college. What a jerk, huh?"

As far as bad boyfriends went, Ryan figured he had

the market cornered. He'd done far worse to Victoria, and now he felt as if he were losing what little closeness he'd begun to develop with their daughter. "Long-distance relationships are tough. Maybe he's worried about never seeing her."

"People can text, Skype, email and talk on the phone."

Was that how his relationship with Kaley was going to be, communicating through technical devices? "That isn't the same as seeing someone."

"June will be coming home on breaks."

He pushed for more. "Maybe you can come to Oregon on your breaks. Then you can see June when she's here on hers. And me, too, of course."

"Sure. I could do that sometimes. But you know what would be nice for now? If I stayed longer on this trip. Would you care if I extended it for another week?"

Would he care? He just about flew over the moon. "I think that's a great idea. There's so much more we can do together, and you can schedule more outings with June when I'm at the clinic."

"Oh, that's right. You'll be going back to work."

"Yes, but I'll still make time for you."

Kaley spoke to Victoria, who was sitting quietly in the leather chair. "Will you stay, too?"

The color drained from Victoria's face. "I don't know, honey."

"Please."

Ryan considered the circumstances. Kaley obviously wanted her birth mother by her side. She hadn't reached a comfort level of being alone with him yet, but she didn't want to go home, either. She'd put Victoria in a quandary. But Ryan figured that was part of being a parent. You did things for your children that you wouldn't do for anyone else.

"Let me think about it," Victoria said.

"All right." Kaley drew her knees up. "But if you don't stay, I'm not sure if I should, either. Then poor Ryan will feel bad." She gave him the same kind of nudge they'd exchanged before. "He'll be lonely without us."

Victoria squinted. "That's not fair, Kaley."

The teen grinned. "What? To blackmail you? What's one more week? You brought enough work with you for a month."

"And I haven't gotten a darn bit of it done, either."

"You will for sure next week with Ryan going back to work, too. It will be like an *almost* normal household. The birth mom and dad at work, and their now—grown-up kid running around playing with her new best friend."

Ryan bit back a laugh. Kaley was good. Damned good.

Victoria shot him a look. "Don't encourage her."

He defended his smirk. "I didn't say anything."

She stuck to her guns. "And I still need to think about it. I'll let you both know sometime tomorrow."

Ryan's heart bumped his chest. The clock was ticking.

Chapter Six

Victoria woke up the next morning with her head buzzing, knowing there was another possible week at stake. She'd been counting down the days until she left, and now Kaley had thrown a wrench into the works. She shouldn't let her daughter do this to her. She should just say no and forget it.

But there were things to consider, like that "blackmail" joke Kaley had made about creating an "almost" normal household.

As funny as the teen was trying to be, the underlying message was clear. Kaley wanted a sense of normalcy, a semblance of family between herself and her birth parents. But Victoria didn't want to stay.

Granted, she wanted to ask Ryan about his ex, but she didn't need an extra week to question him. She could accomplish that today, especially since Kaley would be gone.

Exhausted, she glanced at the clock. Instead of getting up, she closed her eyes, dreading the thought of facing the day. Soon, she fell back asleep.

By the time she reawakened, it was almost noon. Well, hell. She couldn't sleep forever. She dragged herself out of bed and got ready.

She went downstairs, tucked into lazy-day clothes: a plain top, stretch jeans and a battered pair of crocodile-print Doc Martens. All of it had come from a thrift store, but thrifting in L.A. was considered vogue.

She didn't see Ryan or Kaley, so she took a few more minutes to herself. She poured a cup of coffee from a pot that was already made, added her usual cream and sugar, and sipped the satisfying brew. Coffee was the same in the morning or in the afternoon, if it was your first much-needed cup of the day.

She glanced out the kitchen window and noticed it had begun to rain. Now, didn't that figure? Yesterday it was sunny and now it was wet. Oregon, she thought.

A moment later, she heard the front door open. She ventured into the hallway to see Ryan coming into the living room. He looked tall and dark and sort of magical, his hair sprinkled with mist.

"Hey," he said. "You slept in."

She nodded and moved closer. "Where's Kaley?"

"I just dropped her off at June's house. June was going to come over and pick her up, but I offered to take her there instead. I'm trying to get in as much precious parent-time as I can."

Precious parent-time. She certainly couldn't fault him for that. She'd tried to hoard Kaley when she'd first met her, too.

He angled his head, checking out her ensemble. Now

she worried that her stretchy jeans were a little tighter than necessary, but he didn't comment.

He asked her, "So, did you decide if you're staying for another week?"

"No."

"No, you didn't decide or no, you aren't staying?"

"I haven't decided."

"Is there anything I can do to persuade you? Short of begging?"

She clutched her coffee closer to her chest. Did he have to be so gently aggressive? And make her feel so darn confused? "No, there's nothing. I still need a bit more time to mull it over."

He hooked his thumbs in his pockets, reminding her of the boy he used to be. But worse yet was the man he'd become. The man he'd accused her of not seeing for his true self.

"Is it that difficult to be around me?" he asked.

"Truthfully?" She held her cup a little tighter. "It is."

"I wish I could fix how you feel."

And she wished that she'd never loved him. Because now that she was here with him, seeing how much he wanted to be a father, she knew the years she'd spent getting over him were useless. If he took her in his arms and kissed her, she would probably melt like the smitten schoolgirl she once was.

What a mess her emotions were. "I'm going to go back to the kitchen to get a sandwich." She needed to clear her head, to quit thinking about falling prey to his charm.

"I'm hungry, too."

Just her luck, he followed her to the fridge.

They made ham and cheese sandwiches. He opened

the cabinet and removed a box of peanut butter crackers to add to the mix. They each grabbed a banana, too.

He picked up his plate. "Want to eat on the porch with me?" He flashed a trustworthy smile. "I promise I won't pester you about staying."

Her heart skipped. Darn that smile. "Okay. But you better stick to your promise." She didn't want to get pressured into anything.

"I'll be good."

They sat on the weather-beaten chairs out front. She wished that his being good meant that she would stop being affected by his nearness. But that seemed impossible at this point. Good or bad, she was drawn to him.

Trying to distract herself, she gazed at the scenery. There weren't any other houses visible on his street. The rural setting presented fields of green and the ever-present woods. The air smelled sweet and clean and the ground was damp.

She could feel Ryan watching her, and she felt self-conscious being the subject of his quiet attention. She tried to focus on the landscape, but his nearness continued to affect her, making her much too aware of him.

They ate in silence, and afterward he said, "We should go for a walk in the woods like we used to."

She turned to meet his gaze. "Now?"

"Yes, now. We're not doing anything else."

She made a watery motion. "It's raining." And the last thing she needed was to go on a lovely little stroll with him.

"It's drizzling," he countered. "Besides, it will probably stop soon."

"I don't think I should."

"Why? Because your hair might frizz if you step out in it?" He smiled again, teasingly this time.

How many times today would she have to curse his smile? Or fight those old feelings? "I'm not worried about my hair."

"Then what are you worried about?"

Her heart and the way it kept skipping. "Nothing."

"Then walk with me."

Against her better judgment, she gave in. But sitting here making a fuss seemed childish. "A short walk, then I'll be retreating to my room to work." Actually she had plenty of time on her current deadlines, but using it as an excuse seemed safer than being too available.

"That's fine." He stood up. "Ready?"

"I think I should get a hoodie. Just in case."

He chuckled. "Just in case of what? The hair disaster you won't admit that you're worried about?"

"Quit bugging me about my hair."

"I wouldn't have to if you weren't so prissy about it."

"Prissy?" She reached out and mussed up his hair, purposely making it spike.

He playfully grabbed her hand, and suddenly they were behaving like teenagers, flirting and acting silly. She prayed that it didn't inspire the kiss she'd been thinking about earlier. She remembered plenty of kisses in their youth that had started with this type of foolery. She imagined it happening now, and the possibility of a recurrence made her entire body tingle.

Thankfully, it didn't progress. They both let go at the same time, severing the connection.

He said, "It stopped."

She blinked. Was he talking about their attraction?

No, she thought. The drizzle. He was referring to the weather.

She passed on the hoodie, and they descended the porch steps and headed toward the woods.

As they walked side by side, the imagined kiss remained in Victoria's mind. How good it would taste, how exciting it would be to relive the heat from their past.

Determined to destroy her desire, she said, "I asked Sandy what she thought about your ex."

A catch sounded in his voice. "What do you mean? What she thought?"

"Her opinion."

He frowned. "Why does her opinion matter?"

"I was curious about your ex, and Sandy was the only person available to ask, besides you. And I didn't want to get into that type of discussion with you."

"But you're doing it, anyway."

"After a day of contemplation." She hesitated, then added, "You seemed cautious when you mentioned your wife, so I was being cautious, too."

She went silent, putting the ball in his court. But he didn't respond. He merely guided her to their destination, and when they reached the edge of his property, they entered the woods through a break in the trees.

He finally asked, "So what's Sandy's opinion?"

"She said that Jackie seemed nice and that she had a quiet nature. But she also had some concerns about her fidelity."

He stopped walking, a mass of brightly colored leaves towering above his head. "Her fidelity? She didn't cheat on me. I didn't mess around on her, either."

Victoria explained. "Sandy thought it was odd how

quickly she hooked up with someone else after you split, like maybe it had been going on before the divorce."

"There was nothing going on. That wasn't the problem."

"Then what was?"

"I'd prefer not to talk about it."

"Fine. Then keep it to yourself." Flustered, she strode past him, leaving him where he stood.

"Hold on." He caught up with her. "I'm not trying to be difficult. I'm just not used to talking about personal issues. I loved my wife, and it hurt when she left. Sometimes it still hurts."

That wasn't what she'd wanted to hear. But what did she expect? For him to say that he'd married Jackie because he'd secretly loved Victoria and needed someone to replace her? She knew better than to think that was the case. If he'd loved her, even a smidgen, he would have come to the hospital that day.

"You don't have to talk about it," she said. This wasn't a therapy session. It wasn't her job to help him get over his wife.

"Maybe I should tell you." He blew out an audible breath. "Jackie wanted to start a family. That's why she left me."

Confused, she furrowed her brow. "So why didn't you start a family?"

"Because I wasn't ready to be a dad."

"Then why are you pushing so hard to be a father to Kaley?"

"It's different with her. She's the reason I wasn't ready to have a baby with Jackie. How could I bring another life into this world after turning away from the one I already had? If I'd been there when Kaley was born, if I'd done the right thing, it probably wouldn't have been a problem. But as it were, I needed more time to get used to the idea of having other kids. But Jackie got fed up with waiting. She said that she was tired of me using the daughter I'd given up as an excuse not have a family with her."

Wow, Victoria thought. Simply wow. "Maybe to some degree she was right."

He flinched. "How can you say that, knowing that it was Kaley who was in my heart? The same child you mourned? That you searched for?"

"I'm not saying that I don't understand how Kaley affected you, especially with the guilt you've been carting around. But I can see Jackie's perspective." If Victoria had been his wife, she would've wanted his babies, too. "How long was she supposed to wait?"

"Until I was ready."

"And how long was that going to take?"

"Cripes. You sound like Jackie."

"She was your wife. She wanted a future with you."

"And I needed more time to consider fatherhood."

"I know, but—"

"But what? You don't have other kids. You never even got married."

She didn't appreciate the comparison. In fact, it raised her hackles. Especially since she'd worked so hard to forget him, to shed him from her skin, to banish him from her heart. "I already told you, I like being single."

"Do you?" he challenged. "Do you really?"

"Don't turn this around on me. I'm not the one who panics."

"What's that supposed to mean?"

"It means you panicked when I needed you, and you panicked when your wife needed you, too."

"Thanks for the empathy." He made a stabbing motion, as if she'd just knifed him in the heart. He used his fist to push the imaginary blade deeper.

She winced. His marriage had failed because he was remorseful about Kaley, and here Victoria was, punishing him for the years he'd suffered. "I'm sorry. I shouldn't have been judging you or making you feel worse."

He responded in kind. "I shouldn't have been judging you, either. Or making off-the-cuff comments about your choice to remain single."

"We were both being petty. And here of all places." She made a grand gesture, encompassing the trees. When they were young, they'd treated the woods as sacred grounds. But today they'd been using it as a battlefield.

A breeze whispered past them, stirring the air, calling a cease-fire and making her look into his eyes.

He said, "Toward the end, Jackie accused me of not loving her enough. She said that if I'd loved her the way a husband should love his wife, then I would've quit obsessing about the past and had children with her."

This wasn't a good time to discuss the degrees of love, but she listened, lending him her ear.

He continued. "In the beginning of our relationship, she encouraged me to talk about you and the baby. I think my pain appealed to her."

"Most women like the idea of healing a man."

"She was considerate of your pain, too. She used to say that she felt bad for you. She never regarded you as a threat."

"Why would she, after what you told her about me? There was no reason for her to see me as anything except the girl who'd been left at the hospital."

"I'm so sorry I wasn't there for you."

"You don't have to keep apologizing."

"Yes, I do."

He searched her gaze and ignited a spark inside her chest, where her heart was beating much too fast.

She softly said, "I wonder if Jackie knows that Kaley and I are visiting you."

"Someone in town will tell her. But I doubt she'll care. She's happy with her fiancé. From what I heard, they're getting married in the fall, sometime around her birthday."

"Do you think they'll have kids right away?"

"I hope so. She has a right to have the family she wanted. I'm just glad that I have Kaley in my life now. And you."

"I'm not part of your life, Ryan."

"You're part of this moment."

Neither of them broke eye contact. The spark inside her chest hadn't subsided, either. If anything, it grew stronger, along with the rapid cadence of her heart.

"I didn't realize how much I missed you, Victoria."

This was it. The situation she'd feared. He was leaning in to kiss her. She shouldn't allow it to happen. But she reached for him instead, just as he was reaching for her.

Her eyes drifted closed, and as his lips found hers, she became painfully aware of how much she'd missed him. No, that wasn't true. She'd always known.

He slipped his arms around her, drawing her body

against his. She made a soft sound, and their tongues met and mated.

Other men had kissed her this way, but no one ever made her melt except him. It was understandable when she was a teenager, but now? She hadn't learned her lesson. She'd gotten burned and she was back for a second scorching.

But heaven on earth, he tasted good, so potent. Victoria had lost her capacity to reason. All she wanted was more. Hungry, she deepened the kiss, then...

Whoosh! The sky opened up in a gush of rain.

Mother Nature's fury. Clearly, the clouds were shaking their puffy heads in disapproval. The wake-up call Victoria needed. Ryan, too, apparently. They jumped apart and stared at each other for a millisecond.

He grabbed her hand. "Let's go!"

They tore off in the direction of the house, the summer downpour chasing them the entire way, the rain getting harder, their feet sinking into the soil.

Soaked to the bones, they entered his house through the back door and stood in the mudroom. He grabbed a couple of towels that were hanging on hooks and gave her one. But it hardly made a dent. Both of them removed their shoes and socks.

"I told you I needed my hoodie," she said, growling at him like a drowned rat.

He burst out laughing. "Sorry."

"You and your walk in the woods." And his incredible kiss. And his beautiful boyish laughter.

She punched his arm. "Knock it off."

"Doesn't it make you long to move back to the Northwest?"

"Yeah, me and my hair. It's going to take me an hour to fix it." The blow-dryer, the flatiron, the hassle.

"So don't fix it." He waggled his brows. "Pretend we just got out of the shower together and that you want your hair to go wild."

"Oh, right. That's all I need to pretend."

"It was a hell of a kiss."

She pictured Satan nipping at her heels. "I'll probably go to hell for it, too." The sin of sins, she thought. Making out with the man she used to love. "I'm going upstairs to change."

"Not me. I have some extra stuff in here." He reached into a metal trunk crammed with clothes.

Before he got the urge to undress in front of her she said, "My cue to leave."

"Come back, okay?"

"What?"

"Don't stay holed up in your room, working. Hang out with me and I'll make popcorn and root beer floats."

Their favorite snack combination when they were kids. If she burned in hell for this, so be it. "Okay."

"And don't redo your hair."

More hell burning. "All right, but I want an extra scoop of ice cream in my float."

He smiled. "Yes, ma'am."

Victoria left the mudroom and dashed upstairs. She changed into dry clothes and checked her hair in the bathroom mirror. She didn't fix it, per se, but she used a generous dollop of anti-frizz serum, laminating the curls that were already forming. She gave it a quick blast with the blow-dryer, too, making it wilder than it had ever been and sending the curls flying. If she was going to burn in hell, she might as well make it count.

After a hasty application of lip gloss and one last hair fluff, she returned to Ryan. He was in the kitchen waiting for her.

"Lady Victoria." He grinned. "What a scandalous minx you are."

Lady Victoria? He'd never called her that before. Being a scandalous minx was new, too. She swept her gaze over him. He'd changed into jeans and a plaid shirt, which he'd left unbuttoned. "Ryan the Rake made me do it."

He gave a slight bow, mocking a medieval knight. "I should have known you would give me a villainous title."

She did her darnedest not to get distracted by his slightly bared chest or the country-boy fit of his inky blue Wranglers. "If the title fits…"

He put a bag of popcorn in the microwave. While it popped, he prepared the root beer floats.

She watched the drinks foam and fizzle. She watched him lick the side of his glass when it spilled over, too. Lord.

They sat in the living room and snacked. He opened the blinds. The rain had stopped.

"It can't make up its mind," he said.

Neither could she. One minute she wanted to run as far away from him possible, the next she couldn't seem to get enough. "I still don't know what I should do."

"About staying for another week?"

She nodded. "Being here with you scares me."

"What's there to be afraid of?"

Plenty, she thought. Like tumbling back into bed with him. Or, God forbid, falling back in love. "The longer I stay, the higher the odds that I might do something dumb."

"Like what, sleep with me? What's dumb about that?"

"You shouldn't even have to ask me that."

"We're consenting adults now, Victoria."

"Who should know better than to have an affair. If I stay, it will be for Kaley."

"Does that mean you're going to stay?"

Did it? She thought about their daughter and how happy it would make her. "Yes. But I'm not going to slip up and do the unthinkable with you."

No sex. No love. No way.

Chapter Seven

Ryan was grateful that Victoria was staying, because that meant Kaley would stay for sure, too. But he also wished that Victoria saw things differently. He wanted to be with her. He wanted to have the affair she'd rebuffed. He understood that she was afraid. He was the guy who'd hurt her. But the circumstances were different now, and she was stronger, more independent. If anyone got hurt, it could very well be him.

He stirred his root beer float. Most of the ice cream had melted, but there were still a few icy clumps in his glass. "Can I ask you something?"

She glanced up from her drink. "What?"

"I know you prefer being single, but has there ever been anyone special?"

"All of my dates have been casual."

"Which, I assume, means you've been having casual sex, too."

She leveled her gaze at him. "That's not fair."

"I'm just pointing out the obvious."

"Which is?"

"How much you've changed." He studied her in the overcast light. With her fiery red hair tumbling around her face and her green eyes ablaze, she looked like the incarnation of a man-eating succubus. "You're not the same innocent girl you were back then. You're an L.A. woman now. A seductress."

"You're the seductive one, Ryan."

"Really? Well, that's funny because I haven't been with anyone since Jackie left."

She seemed surprised. "Why didn't you date after you got divorced?"

"Because my dad was here, for one thing, and I was trying to help him get well. Then after he died, I was struggling with how that made me feel. Being alone was easier. I guess I just got used to being celibate." Until she'd reappeared in his life, until the desire for her came rushing back.

She put her drink on the table, next to the popcorn they'd been sharing. "Mostly I've been celibate, too."

"What about the casual sex?"

"It's been few and far between."

Pleased, he smiled. He didn't like thinking of her having the naughty time of her life, not unless it was going to be with him. "I'll never forget our first time. I wanted you so badly." He wanted her just as badly now. He ached to devour her, to relish the woman she'd become. "You were so sweet and shy."

"I was nervous. But you weren't."

"Because I had an angel in my bed."

She gave a soft little shiver. "I had no business getting under the covers with you."

"My dad would have killed me if he knew how often we used to fool around in my room when he was at work."

She put her hand on her stomach. "Not to mention that Kaley was conceived during one of those fool-around sessions."

"We weren't very responsible." She'd gotten pregnant because the condom box had turned up empty, and they'd been too eager to stop and think. "I would never forgo the protection now, not unless I was trying to have another child, which we both know isn't my agenda."

"I'm not going to sleep with you, Ryan." She was obviously stopping and thinking now. "I can't get wrapped up in an affair."

Even if she wanted to, he thought. He could feel her pent-up passion, the heat swirling between them.

"I wish it wasn't so complicated," he said.

Her breath hitched. "It wouldn't be if we didn't have a past."

She didn't look like a succubus anymore. She'd morphed back to the innocent girl from their youth. Or maybe she was a bit of both.

After a bout of awkward silence, something they should be used to by now, he said, "I won't mention it again. I won't pressure you." Ryan the Rake had struck out. But he wasn't giving up on spending some quality time with her. "How would you like to learn to milk a cow instead?"

Victoria blinked, smiled. "That's quite a transition from having sex with you."

"We can't just sit here and stare at the walls." And

he wasn't ready to let her slip off to her room to work, either.

"Maybe you should teach me on a day that Kaley is here. You promised to show her. I'd be stealing her thunder if you gave me a lesson first."

"I already showed her this morning while you were asleep."

"Oh, wow. How'd did she do?"

"She was a champ. It was a wonderful experience for both of us." And now he wanted to re-create it with Victoria. "The cow needs to be milked twice a day. So, what do you say, are you game?"

"Why not? If my daughter is becoming a farmer, then I can certainly become one, too."

"This isn't a farm. I have one little cow and a handful of chickens."

"I know. But it's as close to a farm as I'm ever going to get. I'm an L.A. woman. Or so I've been told."

Were they flirting? Or just being friendly? He didn't know, but whatever it was, he wasn't going to mess with success. "Mabel will be thrilled to make your acquaintance, with you being a city girl and all. Especially when I tell her that you're Kaley's mother."

"Mabel is your cow, I presume."

"Yes, but she has dreams of moving to Hollywood and being in a cheese commercial."

Victoria sputtered into laughter. "Mabel tells you her dreams?"

"In secret, so don't let her know that I told you."

"Goodness, and here I thought your name was Dr. Nash, not Dr. Dolittle."

"What can I say? Those were my favorite books

when I was a kid. They might even be what planted the seed for me to want to become a veterinarian."

"Then I'm glad Mabel talks to you."

"Are you ready to meet her?" He stood up and offered a hand.

She took the proffered hand, and for a second, the hunger he'd been suppressing came back. He wanted nothing more than to kiss her.

Their hands drifted apart. If she was feeling the same thing, she pretended otherwise.

She said, "I need to put my boots on."

"So do I." They'd left their shoes by the back door.

They proceeded to the kitchen and into the mudroom. She sat on the edge of the trunk and slipped on her socks.

When she reached for her boots, he said, "So what's the deal? Did Sid Vicious wrestle a crocodile for those?"

"Oh, funny. Dr. Dolittle is making punk rock jokes. And for the record, they're not real crocodile."

"I know." He could tell the difference. "They look good on you, by the way. They work with the hair."

"It's my novelty for the day."

"The boots or the hair?"

"The hair. I wear these boots all the time."

Ryan buttoned his shirt and tucked the tails into his jeans. When he glanced up from his zipper, he noticed that Victoria had finished tying her fake crocodiles and was watching him.

His first thought was: Should he apologize? Then he realized how odd that would be. Who said they were sorry for adjusting their clothes? He continued what he was doing. Finally, she glanced away, as if becoming aware that she'd been staring.

She moved toward the door and waited for him to put on his shoes. "How much milk does Mabel produce?"

"She averages about three gallons a day, a lot less than a full-size cow, but still more than I need."

"What do you do with the excess?"

"I give it to my staff. One of my techs makes yogurt and cheese. Ice cream, too. She made the ice cream I used in our floats. Every so often, she brings me a big batch of vanilla."

"It was delicious."

"She and her husband have a brood of kids. Ice cream comes in handy at their house. The kids help make it, too."

They left the mudroom, and when they passed the chicken coop, he said, "Kaley collected eggs with me this morning. And after we milked Mabel, I showed her how to separate the cream from yesterday's milk, too. It takes a day or so for it to rise."

"She must have been up early to do all of that with you."

"She was."

"Some of the kids we went to school with had farm animals, but I never paid much attention. I guess it's because I grew up in the suburban part of town."

"And I always lived near the woods, even then." He thought about the modest house where he'd been raised. "I always wanted to be on this side of the woods, though." Which was comparable to being on the right side of the tracks, he supposed.

She matched his easy stride. "You've got the best of everything here. You've done well for yourself."

"I'm sure you've done well, too. I'll bet your place in L.A. is nice."

"It is. But it's just an apartment."

"How close do you live to Kaley and Eric?"

"About fifteen miles."

That was certainly close enough to make things convenient, making him wonder what he'd been wondering all along: Would Eric and Victoria eventually become more than friends? The possibility existed, at least in Ryan's mind, and he hated how it made him feel.

They approached the barnyard that doubled as Mabel's pasture, and he forced himself to quit thinking about Victoria pairing up with Eric.

"There she is," he said, as the cow moseyed over to the fence. The fawn-colored mini was all of forty inches tall, with white markings on her face.

"The future TV star." Victoria smiled. "She's adorable."

Mabel lifted her head, as if she actually stood a chance of going to Hollywood.

"She has to be milked on a stand. But there's a platform in her stall that was built for her. The stall itself had to be modified, too." He opened the gate, and they went inside.

"Can I pet her?" Victoria asked.

"Absolutely. She enjoys the attention."

She stroked the side of Mabel's neck. "Obviously you breed her when it's necessary for milk production." She gave the animal another affectionate pat. "I wonder if she misses her calves when they're gone."

"Cows are content when they're pregnant or have a calf. But once their calves are weaned, they do just fine."

"I wanted to nurse Kaley after she was born."

He'd never considered their baby at her breast. But

now that he thought about it, he understood. "Maybe you should have."

"The hospital probably wouldn't have wanted me to. My parents certainly wouldn't have approved. Besides, it would have made giving her up that much harder."

Once again, he understood. "There's nothing stronger than the bond between mother and child."

She nodded. By now, Mabel was gazing at Victoria, the animal's expression seeming sorrowful. But Mabel always had that big wide-eyed look. She was a cow.

He took Mabel to her stall and secured her, focusing on the lesson.

He said to Victoria, "The most important part of this is keeping everything clean."

After they scrubbed their hands, he showed her how to wash Mabel's teats. Then he got two stools and sat beside Victoria, preparing her for the milking. He placed a sanitized bucket under the cow.

"Are you comfortable?" he asked.

"Are you talking to me or Mabel?"

"You."

"I'm fine."

"Are you sure?" After the conversation they'd had, he wanted to be certain that she wasn't sad.

"I'm positive. I want to learn to do this. I like Mabel."

"She likes you, too. But you need to be able to move away quickly if she decides to kick. She never has and I doubt she ever will. But even the nicest cow can kick like a mule."

"That's good to know."

"Some people apply a bit of lubricant to their hands so it lessens the friction."

"Do you want me to do that?"

"Yes. But I'll help you put it on." He knew that she was capable of applying it herself, but he wanted an excuse to touch her.

She extended her hands and he rubbed in the lubricant. She already had soft skin, but now it would be even softer. Suddenly she seemed nervous, and he suspected it was from his proximity, not from the prospect of milking the little cow she'd already begun to like.

He said, "Wrap your hands around two of Mabel's teats. Like this."

He showed her the method he preferred, and she inhaled a choppy breath, still affected by him, presumably.

He explained the motion. "Clamp each teat between your thumb and forefinger and squeeze down to push out the milk. Be gentle, but firm. And maintain your grip so the milk doesn't flow back up into the udder."

She gave it a try and nothing happened.

"You're being too gentle."

"I don't want to hurt her."

"You won't. Not unless you yank instead of squeeze."

"I'd never do that."

"Then try it again."

She made another attempt and squealed when the milk shot out.

Ryan laughed. Kaley had made the same excited sound when she'd first done it, too. "Keep going."

She continued, filling the pail partway. He told her when to switch to the other two teats, and she finished the task.

He praised her accomplishment. "You did a good job."

"Thank you. What do we do with the milk?"

"We're going to strain it to remove any debris that might have gotten in there. We're going to pasteurize it, too. Some people drink it raw, but I prefer to pasteurize."

Hours later, after he'd taught her to complete the processes and they had a bit of dinner, Kaley came home.

She took one look at Victoria and said, "Your hair."

"I got caught in the rain earlier."

"It's crazy wild. I like it."

"Really?" Victoria pulled it back into a ponytail with her hands. "I think I went overboard with the way I styled it."

"I think it's perfect for the rain." Kaley glanced at Ryan. "What do you think?"

"It was my idea for her to wear it that way."

Victoria changed the subject. She asked Kaley, "How was your visit with June?"

"It was totally fun. Oh, and get this? She's going to help me research Ryan's family tree and his Paiute roots. She's a history major, so she's really into it."

"That's great, honey."

Ryan thought it was great, too, except he wished that he was able to teach Kaley about his heritage instead of her having to research it.

Kaley asked Victoria, "What did you guys do, except get caught in the rain?"

"Ryan taught me to milk Mabel."

"Really? That's awesome. Isn't she just the cutest thing?"

As they chatted about the cow and compared milking notes, Ryan wondered what Kaley would think if she knew that her birth parents had kissed today. Not that either of them would ever tell her.

When the Mabel talk ended, Victoria told Kaley that she'd agreed to stay the extra week. The teenager grinned and hugged her.

Kaley then said to Ryan, "Can we start doing some touristy stuff now that we have more time? June told me about Silver Falls. She said it's the biggest state park in Oregon and that they have a hiking trail with a bunch of really beautiful waterfalls. Maybe we can go there? I've never seen a waterfall in person."

"June is right. It's an incredible spot. Why don't we go tomorrow?" He glanced at Victoria. "All of us." He shifted back to Kaley. "You can invite June to come along, too."

"Oh, that would be super. I'm sure she'll want to come with us. She loves that place. Thanks, Ryan." Kaley bounced on her heels. "I'll text her and give her a heads-up. I also need to call Dad and tell him that we're staying for another week."

After she zoomed off, Ryan said to Victoria, "Do you think Eric will care that she extended her trip?"

"I think he'll be glad that she's having a good time."

Ryan was glad, too, happier than he'd ever been. Except for the sweet, hot frustration of wanting Victoria again.

Immersed in nature, Victoria walked beside Ryan on an eight-plus-mile hike that showcased ten spectacular waterfalls, some of which were over a hundred feet high.

Kaley and June had walked on ahead, promising to meet at a designated area, where the four of them were going to picnic later.

Ryan said, "I'm glad June knows this trail so well.

Otherwise I wouldn't have been comfortable letting her and Kaley go off by themselves."

"Me, either, especially with the way the trail narrows and drops off in spots." Of course there were shortcuts for less experienced hikers that led back to the parking lot, but Victoria appreciated that Ryan had become such a protective parent. The days she'd spent in Oregon so far had changed her perspective about him, and she still had over a week left to go.

How changed would she be by then?

They continued walking, surrounded by grassy knolls and moss-covered timber. As the path they'd been concerned about grew tighter, they were forced to move closer together.

When the next fall appeared, they stopped to admire the way it curved and flowed. The motion seemed powerful yet somehow delicate, compared to some of the others they'd seen.

Mesmerized, Victoria stood reverently.

"Wow." Ryan's voice sounded gruffly beside her. "It seems so inviting. Can you imagine playing in it?"

She turned and accidentally skimmed his hand. "What?"

"You know, splashing, kissing—"

"That isn't allowed."

"I know. I'm just saying what an incredible fantasy it would be."

She didn't need to conjure that type of image. But as the overspray misted her face and dampened her eyelashes, her mind strayed in that unholy direction. It would so easy to kiss Ryan now, to tug him closer, to taste the illicit flavor of his lips.

So easy. So hard. So dangerous.

She'd already made that mistake in the woods. She took a step back, moving much quicker than necessary and causing a loose stone to fly out beneath her foot, where the ground was wet.

"Careful." He reached out to steady her.

But it didn't help. His touch sent shock waves through her skin. "You're not supposed to be pressuring me."

"What are you talking about?"

"To have sex."

"I wasn't."

"You put a fantasy in my head."

"Make-believe kisses in a waterfall? That's hardly pressure."

She begged to differ. "It wasn't necessary to say it. Not after the talk we had."

"Then forget I mentioned it."

Forget a scenario that gave her sexy goose bumps? It was probably all she was going to think about for the rest of the day.

Sure enough, that was her fate. Every waterfall on the trail made her want to kiss him, to hold him, to press against the warmth of his body. Even meeting up with the Kaley and June didn't help ease her desire.

As they gathered for their picnic beneath a big shady tree, with a light breeze rustling the leaves, Victoria couldn't quit watching Ryan. The way he stretched out his legs, smiled, talked to the girls, ate his food.

She reminded herself why being attracted to him was a waste of energy and how she would be a fool to act on those feelings. She pounded it into her skull, insisting that she knew better.

But nothing made a difference. No amount of self-

Chapter Eight

Two days later, Victoria stood quietly while Kaley packed. Kaley had arranged an impromptu sleepover at June's. The girls wanted to work on Ryan's side of the family tree and try to uncover more information about his mother. No doubt they also wanted to stay up late, eat loads of junk and enjoy their freedom. June's parents had gone out of town on a business trip, leaving her by herself or in this case, with Kaley as her guest.

June sat on the edge of the bed, waiting. Ryan was in the room, too, fussing over the teenagers like father goose.

"Behave yourselves," he said.

"Seriously?" Kaley crammed a brightly colored top into her overnight case. "We're doing research."

"Yeah, well, I used to tell my dad I was going to the library when I was with Victoria."

"The library." June laughed and drew her knees up,

clearly comfortable in her own skin. "That's not a very believable excuse."

"Yes, it was. I didn't have a PC at home then, and I used to go to the library to use their computers."

"Gosh, that must have been the Dark Ages." Kaley teased him, waving her iPad as she packed it.

"Smarty." He grinned. "Just wait until you have kids and they grow up. They'll think your era was old school, too."

"Because it will be." She zipped her bag. "I'll see you guys sometime tomorrow. Probably in the evening."

"That's when my folks are coming back," June said, climbing off the bed.

"Have fun," Victoria told them, her mind nervously somewhere else. With Kaley gone, she and Ryan would be completely alone. Doomed and alone, with nowhere to hide.

All she'd been doing since the waterfall fantasy was thinking about how much she wanted him.

So why not cave in to temptation? After all, she was older and wiser now. Surely, she was capable of sleeping with Ryan without stumbling back in time. Sex wasn't love, and she wasn't a teenager with a moony heart. She was a strong, independent woman, and if she wanted to let off a little steam with a man from her past, then why the heck not?

Brave thoughts for a woman whose knees were suddenly knocking. With Ryan by her side, she followed the girls downstairs and stood at the front door, watching them drive away in June's Mini Cooper.

He frowned. "I hope they don't get any brilliant ideas and invite some boys over."

"I trust them." A lot more than she trusted herself.

She was mere seconds away from telling him what was on her mind.

"I guess I'm just worried because I'm a guy, and I know how guys can be."

"It isn't Kaley you need to be worried about." She closed the front door. "It's me."

He shot her a sideways glance. "Why? Are you going to invite some boys over?"

"There is one boy I'm considering." One tall, dark man. She figured it was now or never to take the plunge, to dive into the forbidden. "I want to have the affair we talked about. A good time between old lovers."

He kept looking at her, only with skepticism. "When did you decide this?"

"Just now."

"What happened to your reservations? Doing something dumb? Doing the unthinkable with me?"

"I changed my mind. But if you think it's a bad idea…"

"I didn't say that. You just blew me away, that's all. I wasn't expecting this."

He definitely seemed interested, but confused, too, as if trying to process her decision. She liked that she'd caught him off guard. It gave her a sense of control, of making the affair happen on her terms.

She said, "If we do this, we need to be discreet. I don't want Kaley to know."

"You want us to sneak around?"

"I understand how that sounds, but considering the circumstances, it makes more sense. It isn't as if we're going to embark on a long-distance relationship after I leave. All we'll be doing is having a fling while I'm here, and that isn't something we should bring to our daughter's attention. It's our responsibility to set a proper example."

"By sneaking around?"

"I'm just trying to protect her."

"I know, and I'll abide by your wishes."

She reiterated. "We can be together whenever Kaley is gone somewhere with June, but never when she is here. I won't be creeping into your room at night while our daughter is asleep under the same roof."

"Okay." He agreed once more.

She fought for her next breath. Nervous again. Was she really going to strip down with him? She ran her gaze over the long lean length of his denim-clad body. Yes, by heavens, she was.

He tugged a hand through his hair, spiking the dark strands, then smoothing them, then spiking them again. "I think I should wine and dine you first."

She started. "What?"

"Take you on a date. We should go out tonight."

"That isn't necessary." She didn't want to make more of this than it was.

"It's absolutely necessary."

"No, really—"

He cut her off. "I'm not going to just haul you upstairs and have sex, Victoria. We're going to do this right. Dinner, dancing, moonlight kisses. Women like that stuff. *You* like that stuff. Remember how badly you wanted me to take you to the junior prom?"

Yes, she remembered. But by the time prom rolled around, she was pregnant and showing and felt stupid and scared. "That's water under the bridge."

"Did you go to your senior prom when you were in California?"

"No." She dared to ask. "Did you go to yours here?"

"God, no. All I cared about then was getting out of high school, not celebrating one of the loneliest years of my life. So let's fix that, shall we? Let's get gussied up and have ourselves a prom-type date. I'll even buy you a corsage."

Her heart pounded with long-lost expectation, a girlish excitement she couldn't deny. But still, she protested. "This affair is supposed to be about moving forward. Not going back in time."

"We *are* moving forward. We're replacing bad memories with good ones, like we did at the hospital."

Instead of continuing the debate, she gave in. "Are you going to wear a tux?"

"No. But I'll wear a nice black suit. I've got one in the closet."

"I didn't bring any evening dresses with me. I'm going to have to shop."

"There's a new mall in Meadow Creek. I've never been there, but I heard it's nice."

Meadow Creek was about thirty miles away. "I'll give it a try." As long she'd agreed to do this, she wanted to find the perfect dress.

"Call me when you buy something."

"Why?"

"So you can tell me what color it is and I can have the florist make a corsage to go with it."

For two people who were moving forward, this felt a lot like high school. "Get yourself a boutonniere to match, too."

"I will."

"I'll pay you back for it."

"You don't have to do that."

"The boutonniere is the girl's responsibility."

"Okay." He smiled. "Now go and shop. I need to make the dinner reservation. I need to figure out where we can go dancing, too. Someplace nicer than the local bars."

"Good luck with that."

"I'll find a place."

Such confidence. She liked that quality in a man. She liked him. But loving him was another story. She wasn't going to fall into that trap, no matter how romantic their evening turned out to be.

She got directions to the mall, grabbed her purse and hit the road.

Once she was at the mall, she milled in and out of stores. She tried on a boatload of dresses, but nothing appealed to her. They were either too frilly, too simple, too bridesmaidsy, too young, too matronly, too skimpy, too sequined, not shiny enough. She found fault with everything.

Was that an indication that she was finding fault with herself? Was she the problem?

No, dang it. It was simply a case of struggling to find the right outfit.

Finally, she uncovered her prize: a gold mini dress, with a sweetheart neckline and a floor-length chiffon overskirt.

She stood in front of the mirror in the fitting room, pleased with her reflection. The thigh-high length was alluring, and the slit-up-the-side overskirt provided a hint of mystery, flowing as she moved. The color complemented her hair and skin tone, and the bareness of the neckline was sleek and ladylike, without revealing too much cleavage.

Holy mother, she was excited. This really did feel like prom night, only with an adult edge. An affair, she thought, eighteen years in the making. She needed this. Ryan needed it. Being together in this manner was the right thing to do.

Victoria purchased the dress and hunted down gold pumps and an evening bag to top off the look. She shopped for jewelry as well, zeroing in on a pair of earrings that dangled softly.

That was it! She was done.

No, wait. It wouldn't hurt to buy new lingerie. This was an affair, after all, a night that would end in fireburning lust and a tangle of unclothed bodies.

Her body. His body.

Already she was feeling the effect.

She chose a nude strapless bra and nude panties. Pure. Classic. An eloquent statement beneath the shimmery dress.

On her way down the escalator, she caught sight of the fragrance counter.

And within no time she purchased a luxurious body lotion. And, yes, it was vanilla scented. She couldn't seem to help herself. She wanted Ryan to breathe in the type of fragrance that had aroused him when they were young.

Remembering that she'd promised to call, she sat on a bench inside the mall, with her packages next to her, and phoned him.

He answered right away. "Hey. How's it going?"

"Great. My dress is shiny and gold."

"That sounds fetching."

"I'm looking forward to tonight."

"Me, too. I've got everything arranged. Dinner is at eight."

She glanced at her watch. She had plenty of time. "I'm on my way home now."

"See you."

"You, too."

After she ended the call, she realized that she'd called his house "home." But it wasn't her home. She shrugged it off as a figure a speech. She wasn't going to overanalyze. Not tonight. She was simply going to enjoy herself.

She headed to the parking lot, piled her purchases into her rental car, started the engine and sped off.

On the open stretch of highway, she blasted the radio, singing along to Katy Perry, then Maroon Five, then Rihanna. Kaley had set the dial when they'd first arrived in Oregon. Victoria smiled, thinking about the pop tunes that she and Ryan used to favor.

Thirty-some miles later, she arrived at the farmhouse. She went inside and Ryan greeted her.

"Can I see your dress?"

She clutched the garment bag. "Not until I'm wearing it."

"Tease." He smiled, ever the charmer. "I ordered the flowers. But I haven't picked them up yet. Do you want me to grab some takeout for you while I'm out? A snack before the main meal tonight?"

"No, thanks. I'm good. I had a burger at the mall."

"Then I'll go the florist and see you when I get back."

"No, you won't. Not for a while. I'm going to soak in the tub and relax naked on my bed before it's time to get ready."

He swallowed, and his Adam's apple bobbed. "Now

you're really being a tease." A long silence passed before he said, "Are you really going to do that?"

Using her feminine wiles, she played coy. "Do what?"

"Lie naked on your bed?"

"Yes, I really am." She turned and went upstairs with her purchases and a slight sway of womanly hips, knowing he was watching.

At seven-fifteen Ryan waited in the living room for Victoria. He was dressed and ready to go, with the corsage and boutonniere boxes handy. If this had been their real prom, he would have been sitting here at her parents' mercy and being scrutinized by them. But he was just as nervous, he realized.

He was thrilled, too, that they were going the distance. There wasn't a woman in this world he would rather have an affair with than Victoria. He still had mixed feelings about keeping it a secret from Kaley, though. He understood and respected Victoria's reasoning, but he suspected that it was going to be awkward when Kaley was around and they were trying to behave as if they weren't being intimate or didn't have romantic feelings for each other.

But they would cross that bridge when they came to it. Besides, it was only for a week. They wouldn't have to keep the pretense going forever.

When Victoria entered the room, he jumped up and grabbed the corsage box. She was an absolute vision. The gold dress was a knockout. Everything about her was spectacular. Her hair was straight and smooth, and although she'd pinned it up, little pieces were falling.

He assumed she'd done that deliberately. She was also wearing a wildly sexy shade of red lipstick.

"You look like a goddess," he said.

"Thank you. You look incredibly handsome, too."

"Thanks." He'd paired his suit with a white shirt and black tie, keeping it traditional. He opened the clear container and showed her the corsage. It was a white rose, sprinkled with gold glitter and adorned with a gilded ribbon.

"That's beautiful, Ryan. It's perfect."

"Can I slip it on you?"

"Of course." She extended her wrist.

After it was in place, they gazed at each other, and his heart started beating faster than he would have liked. But he couldn't seem to make it slow down, so he let it run wild, like everything else they were going to do tonight. "Do you want to put the boutonniere on me?"

She nodded, and he got the flower and handed to her. She pinned it onto his lapel the way a teenager might, fumbling with the effort. She was obviously as nervous as he was.

"This is what we would have done years ago," he said. "Only your parents would have been taking pictures."

"Not happily, though."

"No. They were never happy when I came to pick you up for a date."

She fussed with the boutonniere. "It's crooked. I need to redo it."

She moved closer and started over, and suddenly he could smell the fragrance on her skin.

"You're wearing the sweet stuff you used to wear."

"It's not the same brand."

"It's having the same effect." He wanted to eat her alive.

"I was hoping it would."

"You hoped right." Later he was going to lead her to his bed and devour her like the cupcakes they'd made. "We better get going." Before he lost control and carried her upstairs.

"Your boutonniere isn't ready yet." She fussed a bit more and fixed it. "Now we can go."

They drove quietly, until she said, "Where are you taking me?"

"It's a new place that serves Mediterranean food. The cuisine is exceptional and the atmosphere is the nicest in town." He explained further. "I know the owner from the chamber of commerce. He's on the board of directors. When I called to make the reservation, I talked directly to him and asked if he could arrange for us to have one of his best tables. I told him my old girlfriend was visiting from California and I wanted to take her on a fancy reunion date."

"What did he say?"

"That he would treat us like royalty."

She smiled. "It pays to know people in high places."

"He'd already heard about you through the gossip mill. And about Kaley, too."

"Word travels fast."

"People like to talk, especially in small towns."

"This town isn't that small."

"It's small enough."

Soon they entered the lavishly decorated restaurant. It wasn't overly crowded since it was a weeknight, but the other patrons noticed them just the same. Because of Victoria, Ryan thought, and her stunning gold ensemble.

The owner, whose name was Isa, led them to their table, which was a candlelit booth draped with a lush silk curtain and jeweled tiebacks.

Victoria complimented him on his establishment, and he thanked her kindly. He recommended a dry, neutral wine to accompany the richly spiced dishes.

The evening went splendidly. They dined on a variety of delicious appetizers and salads that Isa provided with pride. The main course was also carefully selected by their host.

"This is wonderful," Victoria said to Ryan. "I don't think I've ever been on a nicer date. We really are being treated like royalty."

He smiled, enjoying her company and basking in her compliment. "The king and queen of a miniature-cow farm?"

"With only one cute little cow." She laughed. "If Mabel could see us now she would be impressed."

"And rightly so."

She glanced around. "Too bad they don't have a dance floor here."

"Don't worry. I found a place that will accommodate us for that."

She leaned forward. "Where?"

"You'll see when the time comes."

After they finished their meal, an impressive array of pastries was served, along with exotic-flavored coffee.

As they lingered over dessert, he said, "I'm never going to forget this night."

"It's going to remain forever in my mind, too."

And they were just getting started, Ryan thought.

He studied her, jolted by the heat, the erotic sensations. As he gazed at her mouth, she moistened her lips. "What's that called?" he asked.

"What's what called?"

"The name of your lipstick?"

"Crimson honey."

"And what's the name of your perfume?"

"It's body lotion. And it's called vanilla sugar."

Crimson honey and vanilla sugar. It didn't get any more luscious than that. Sweet beauty.

With the woman of his grown-up dreams.

Chapter Nine

Dinner ended, but Ryan didn't take Victoria to the next location. He took her back to his house instead. Confused, she asked, "Did you forget something?"

"No."

"Then what are we doing here? Did you change your mind about dancing?" Was he cutting the date short so he could get her into bed sooner?

"I haven't changed my mind about anything."

"Do you have something sneaky planned?"

"Maybe."

No maybe about it. He was taking her on a detour. They exited the truck and went into the house.

He led her through the back door, and the moment they stepped onto the patio, she gave a little gasp. He'd decorated with strings of twinkling lights, paper lanterns, and gold and white balloons, creating an idyllic setting. On the table, amid sparkling confetti and a tall white candle, were two crystal flutes.

"The champagne is in the fridge," he said. "We wouldn't have had champagne at our real prom, not legally anyway, but I figured we could have it now." He indicated the stereo he'd set up. "I downloaded a bunch of music from our era, slow songs and ballads to keep it romantic."

"Did you do all of this when I was at the mall?"

He nodded. "It seemed like an easy enough surprise because I figured you wouldn't have any reason to come outside after you got back. Plus, I went crazy trying to find a fancy place for us to go dancing around here, and then it hit me that I should just create our own place. Our own prom, here at home."

"This is beautiful. Thank you." She leaned forward to hug him.

He wrapped her in his arms, and they held each other. He sought her lips, and they kissed with warmth and tenderness. She deepened the exchange, and he reacted, tugging her tighter against him. She welcomed the dizzying heat, the feel-good pressure of his body aligning with hers.

After they separated, they caught their breaths in lung-expanding unison.

"Should we have the champagne now?" he asked.

She nodded. She wanted to celebrate their affair, to throw caution to the wind, to enjoy every wild romantic minute of it.

Ryan went inside to get the bottle. He returned with the cork already popped. He filled the flutes and handed her one. "To the girl from my past."

She clanked his glass with her own, and the crystal chimed. "And the boy from mine."

While they sipped, they looked into each other's eyes.

"No one has ever done anything this special for me before," she said.

"No one ever hurt you the way I did, either."

"You're helping me heal from that." And making love with him tonight was going to be part of her therapy. When this was over, she intended to go home with a newfound sense of calm and confidence.

He leaned in to kiss her again, and she sighed. By next week, it would be over. But for now, she was part of his world: the renovated farmhouse, the animals in his care, the woods with its looming shadows and enchanted beauty.

She said, "I wonder if they're watching us."

"Who?"

"The wood nymphs, fairies and trolls. The creatures that live out there." She'd always liked to pretend that they were real.

"Being watched by wood nymphs sounds sexy." He stepped back to study her. "You could actually be one of them."

"I feel like a nymph tonight." Sensual and free.

"Do you want to dance now?"

"Yes." She wanted to sway in his arms under the twinkling lights, under the moon, under the stars.

He turned on the stereo, playing the music he'd chosen. The first song that came on was Eric's Clapton's acoustic track "Change the World."

He swept her into his arms, and they exchanged a

smile. He'd obviously remembered how much she liked this song.

She said, "When I was driving home from the mall, I was reminiscing about the music we used to listen to, and now I'm dancing with you to one of my favorite songs."

"It's funny how music can take people back to events in their lives, good and bad."

"This is definitely good." An event to treasure.

Song after song, they danced. And kissed. And danced. When they were both ready to go upstairs, it was unspoken between them. They just seemed to know.

He turned off the stereo, and they went to his bedroom. Up until now, Victoria hadn't been in his room. She hadn't even poked her head in when he wasn't around. She'd purposely steered clear of his sleeping domain.

But this was it. The place where they were going to make uncommitted love. She took in her surroundings, taking special notice of the bed, of course. It was neatly made, with a darkly printed quilt. She became aware of the adjoining bathroom, too, which was equipped with a vintage tub and a modern shower.

"Take your dress off," he said. "Let me see you remove it."

She felt suddenly shy. But buried within that shyness was a woman who wanted to boldly bare herself to him.

He turned down the bed and sat on the edge of it, watching her with an intense expression.

She started with her earrings, removing them from her ears and placing them on the dresser. Next came her pumps. Then her dress. It zipped up the side, making it easy to open and slide down her body. The chiffon overskirt pooled as it went lower, until the entire garment landed on the floor in a gold heap.

Wearing nothing but her new bra and panties, Victoria stood before him, waiting for another sensual command.

Preparing for their union, he stripped down to his birthday suit. Her pulse pounded with the jagged craving that came with wanting him. He was a sight for hungry eyes, with his lean muscles and natural athleticism.

He beckoned her. "Come lie down with me."

Eager to get closer to him, she climbed into bed, and he unhooked her bra.

"Victoria," he said softy.

Her breasts spilled free. "Call me Tore."

"I thought I wasn't supposed to do that."

"Tonight you can." Tonight she was breaking all the rules.

He reached into her panties and whispered, "Tore."

She arched her body toward him, and he slipped a finger between her damp folds. As he rubbed in soft little circles, lovely little chills snaked through her blood.

He intensified the sweet pressure, drawing her deeper into the feeling, and she clutched the sheets. Breathless and moaning, she floated on the edge of ultimate pleasure.

He kissed her, his tongue swirling with hers, the taste of him filling her senses.

More edge. More silky sensations.

She was actually in bed with Ryan Nash. She was actually letting him have his beautiful way with her.

"I can't believe this is happening," he said, obviously having the same thought. "You and me."

She jerked her hips. He was oh-so-good with his hands. "Don't stop."

"I wouldn't dream of it."

But he did stop. After she shuddered and shook, after she lay there with her panties askew and her heart skittering, he withdrew his touch.

Good thing, too, because she needed a minute to get her sex-starved bearings. She could have been sixteen again, steeped in her first orgasm.

She closed her eyes, but even so, she could feel him watching her, as if he were trying to read her mind.

Suddenly his lips landed lightly against hers, and like a storybook prince he kissed her. But he wasn't a fairy-tale hero. He was the flesh-and-blood boy who'd broken her heart.

Shutting out the past, Victoria wrapped her arms around her lover, and they rolled over the bed, the kiss getting hotter.

Once she was pinned tightly beneath him, and he held her arms above her head, she opened her eyes. Heavens, he was sexy. His hair fell across his forehead, and the overhead light showcased his golden-bronzed skin.

"I have to get the protection," he said.

Victoria nodded. He was fully aroused. She could feel the hardness.

He released his hold on her, reached into the nightstand drawer and removed a condom.

Riiiip. She heard the package tear.

While he fitted the latex in place, she wondered what he would say if she told him that she'd wanted to marry him when they were young.

He turned back to her, and their gazes locked. "Are you okay?" he asked.

"Why wouldn't I be?"

"You look like you have something troubling on your mind. Are you sure you want to do this? That you're not regretting it already?"

"I don't have any regrets." Not about being in bed with him tonight. But nonetheless she couldn't tell him what she'd been thinking about.

"Good. Because I need to touch you some more." He peeled her panties off for good. He also licked the tips of her breasts, whispering about how pretty and pink her nipples were. He used to say things like that when they were younger, too.

The lovely little chills from earlier returned, especially when he went lower and kissed between her legs.

Heat. Intimacy.

She tunneled her fingers through his hair, tugging, trying to keep her knees from going weak.

If he didn't stop, she was going to shudder and shake again. But that was exactly what he wanted, she realized, to keep her on the frenzied edge of lust.

His mouth. His tongue.

It was all too much. She was losing the battle. And he was winning. The powerful male, claiming his prize.

He reared up and thrust into her. Just like that, they were joined in sexual matrimony. She didn't mean to use that description, but those were the words that zoomed into her mind.

Everything was zooming, spinning in glorious circles. He was braced above her, taking her higher and higher, and keeping his gaze locked on hers.

Victoria didn't know whether to mewl like a kitten

or claw and scratch like a feral cat. She ultimately did both. Soft throaty sounds. Nail marks down his back.

"Cripes," he said, his tone hot and ragged. "I like the way you move."

She was merely following his lead, matching him stroke for stroke, every passionate nerve ending in her body calling out to him. Needing more, she dragged him down for a kiss, and their mouths came together in an explosion of carnal bliss.

They made hot hammering love, right up to the moment of frantic fruition.

In the aftermath, he collapsed on top of her, and she wrapped her arms around him.

Content in the feeling.

Once Ryan regained his stamina, he went into the bathroom to dispose of the condom. Upon his return, Victoria was sitting up in bed with the sheet loosely draped around her.

He took a second to admire her before he said, "How would you feel about a second glass of champagne?"

She smiled. "To toast what we just did?"

"Why not?" He felt like celebrating. "All I have to do is run downstairs and grab the bottle and our glasses."

"Sure. Go ahead."

He lifted his trousers off the floor and zipped into them. "Should I throw some cheese and crackers together, too?"

"You're hungry? After that big fancy meal we had earlier?"

"What can I say?" He shot her a decidedly male grin. "I worked up another appetite."

"Then by all means, fix yourself a snack."

"I'll bring extra for you, just in case." Unable to help himself, he approached the bed and crawled onto the covers to plant a quick kiss on her delectable lips. "I'll be back in a flash."

He left the room, descended the stairs and went outside to gather the champagne supplies and bring them into the kitchen. To make sure the bottle stayed chilled, he put it on ice. He rinsed out the flutes, too, and dried them off. Next he created a simple cheese and cracker platter.

Pleased that he had a woman waiting for him in bed, he smiled to himself. It wasn't just any woman. It was Victoria. Their affair was turning out to be damned fine.

He carried his bounty back upstairs, making two trips. She was right where he'd left her, warm and cozy in bed.

Soon he was seated beside her, with the food platter between them. Each of them sipped from a full glass of bubbly.

Ryan snacked while he drank.

"That does look rather tempting," she said, and helped herself to a cracker and a slice of cheddar. "I guess my appetite is returning, too."

"Good. Because you're going to need the fuel."

"What for?"

"A second round."

She batted her lashes. Miss Innocent. "Of what?"

"You know of what."

"So the sex isn't over for the night?" She fanned herself like a Southern belle. "How wonderfully bad of us."

He turned serious. "You know what I just realized?

That this is the first time we're going to actually spend a full night together."

"I know. It's nice, isn't it? To be able to wake up in the same bed? I dreamed of that when we were young."

"You did?"

"Of course I did. I'm a girl. We're wired for cuddling." She seemed to be studying him now.

"Why are you looking at me like that?" he asked, feeling the weight of her scrutiny.

"I was just thinking about something."

"What?"

She topped off her champagne, paused, sipped. "Do you think you'll ever get married again?"

The question troubled him. He didn't like discussing this type of stuff. "I have no idea."

She went quiet, as if formulating her own opinion. Then she said, "I don't think you will."

Should he ask her to elaborate? No, he shouldn't. But he did anyway. "What makes you say that?"

"I think there was more to your failed marriage than just the kid issue."

He should have seen this coming; he should've known she would take this route. "You think I'm incapable of giving myself fully to someone?"

"You panicked when Jackie needed you, and you claimed to have loved her. That doesn't bode well for commitment."

"Just as me not showing up at the hospital proves how easily I panic? Didn't we already have a conversation like this before?"

"I'm sorry. I wasn't trying to stir an argument."

"We're not arguing." But now that she'd brought up the marriage issue, he turned the tables on her. "So, what about you, Tore? Do you think you'll ever settle down?"

"I honestly don't know." She heaved a sigh. "After all of this time, maybe I'm commitment phobic, too."

He disagreed. "You told me earlier tonight how you were starting to heal from the past. That doesn't sound like a woman who won't be able to commit."

"Oh, that's nice. Thank you." She looked into his eyes. "Now I feel badly for saying what I said about you."

"It's okay. I suppose that the idea of getting remarried does tend to make me feel a little shaky." Even now, he felt unsteady. "I'd never make that kind of commitment again unless I was sure I could handle it."

"I'm glad we were able to talk about this without arguing."

Ryan moved the food platter out of the way, needing to get close to her. He was going to miss the hell out of her when she was gone. "I just want you to be happy."

"I want you to be happy, too."

He had no idea what his future entailed, except that he would be in Oregon and she would be in California. "Promise me that you won't rush into it."

"Rush into what?"

"Marriage."

"Why would I? I don't even have anyone in my life. Except you, and this is only temporary."

"Just don't take the first guy who comes along. No matter how perfect he seems."

"I won't."

"Men can fool you into thinking they're perfect."

"I'm beyond getting fooled." She put her hand against

his cheek. "Now stop telling me what to do. I'm not going to become an impulsive bride."

"I hope not." In spite him wanting her to be happy, he couldn't bear to think of her belonging to another man.

Confused, he kissed her, making sure that his mouth sizzled against hers.

She reacted with an equal dose of hard-edged passion, and they tumbled into each other's arms, preparing for the second round.

With no more talk of marriage.

In the morning Ryan watched Victoria sleep. She remained naked, and her eye makeup from last night was delicately smeared. She hadn't removed it before they'd crashed out, and the effect was softly haunted, creating shadows that weren't real.

Wanting to touch her, to feel the texture of her skin, he skimmed his thumb along her jawline. Unfortunately, that was all it took to wake her. Her eyes fluttered open, and she gazed at him with a baffled expression.

"Sorry," he whispered. "Go back to sleep."

"What time is it?" Her voice was groggy.

"Early." He didn't see the point in reciting the exact hour. "Go back to sleep," he coaxed again.

She squinted at him. "You're already dressed."

"I have chores to do. Then I'm going to come back and take a shower."

"Can I do that with you?"

"The chores?" He smiled. "Or the shower?"

"Both." She sat up and arched her back, stretching her languid body. "I'll hurry and throw myself together."

She gathered her belongings and padded to her room, and he waited for her.

She'd taken the gold dress, her underwear, her shoes and her purse. But she'd forgotten her earrings. Ryan noticed them on the dresser. He had the notion to keep them, to tuck them away in his drawer, but he didn't. Having an affair with her didn't give him the right to take trophies or start a hidden shrine.

Victoria returned about five minutes later, with her hair in a ponytail and her face scrubbed clean. She'd donned a lightweight T-shirt, loose-fitting jeans and the Sid Vicious footwear. He figured they were the closet thing she had to work boots. She looked cute and fresh and younger than her thirty-odd years.

He picked up the earrings and handed them to her. "You forgot these."

"Thanks." She tucked them into a front pocket of her jeans.

"I have the usual animal chores," he said, letting her know what was on the list. "But I also need to clean up the patio from last night's prom."

"I'll be sorry to see the decorations go."

"Paper lanterns don't last forever."

"The twinkling lights have staying power."

"True, but they don't fit my usual style."

"They fit mine. If I lived here for good, I would keep them up." She quickly added, "Not that I plan on staying. I didn't mean that the way it sounded."

"I didn't think you did." Not after the conversation they had last night.

They went outside, and he got a ladder and began removing the lanterns and lights. She took care of the balloons and cleared the table, scooping the confetti into a trash bag.

"What should I do with the candle?" she asked. "Where should I put it?"

"I don't know. I bought it for the ambience, but we didn't even light it."

"Can I put it in my room? It would be nice to have a candle in there."

"Sure. Go ahead."

She sniffed the wax. "Did you know it was scented?"

"No." He hadn't paid attention when he'd purchased it. He'd been in a hurry, grabbing things and tossing them into his cart. "What does it smell like?"

"Gardenia, I think. Definitely floral."

He smiled from his perch on the ladder. He was just finishing up. "Then you keep it for sure."

"I'll take it upstairs now."

She left, and when she returned, they focused on the rest of the chores, tending to the dogs, the chickens and the cow.

A short while later, they moved on to the horse.

Victoria fussed over the gelding, letting him eat from her hand while Ryan mucked the stall.

"What's his name?" she asked.

"Thor."

"Oh, I like that. He's certainly big enough to be a Norse god."

"This Thor was used to haul lumber. That was his job when he was younger and stronger."

"There's legend about Thor the god and a sacred oak tree. I'll bet this Thor knows about it."

Ryan stopped working long enough to appreciate

the way the fiery-haired woman and the ancient equine were connecting. "You make a nice pair."

"He's a big old baby." She fed him another handful of grain. "Aren't you, sweetie?"

The horse bobbed his head, as if to say, "Yes."

Ryan teased her. "Now who's talking to the animals?"

"Me." She laughed. "Are you about ready for that shower, Dr. Dolittle?"

"As long as my trusty lady assistant will be joining me."

"She absolutely will."

"Then I'm ready." He put away his rake and dusted his hands on his jeans, more than happy to get clean with her.

Chapter Ten

Victoria drenched herself under the spray. The water pressure was exquisite, and so was being naked with Ryan.

She offered him his turn under the spray, and he soaked himself down. Once they were both deliciously wet, they took turns with the soap, washing each other's bodies.

She made him hard, deliberately so, lathering his nether regions in a stroking motion. He repaid the favor, taking extra care with her erogenous zones. They moved sideways and did their darnedest to share the water, rinsing in sexy intervals.

Steam fogged the enclosure, like mist from a waterfall.

A waterfall. This definitely bordered on that fantasy, especially when he nudged her toward the shower wall and kissed her.

Hot and sexy. Deep and spiraling with need. She could've kissed him for the rest of her life and never tired of it.

The rest of her life? Victoria shook away the thought. She knew better than to let those long-ago notions interfere with their affair.

Instead, she focused on her healing, on the woman she was becoming, letting it sweep her into erotic oblivion. Ryan's mouth possessed hers, and his hands were everywhere, the water foaming and bouncing between them.

Together, they were making sensual magic. Together, they were locked in carnal passion.

He spoke roughly against her ear. "I forgot to grab a condom. I'll just have to do other things to you."

He was already doing other things, dropping to his knees as he spoke. Enthralled, she looked down at him. She ran her hands through his waterlogged hair. The steam was getting thicker, and so was her hunger.

Victoria made soft moaning sounds. She couldn't help it. He knew how to bring her to ecstasy. It happened quickly, mindlessly, her pulse bumping along the way.

In the aftermath, she nearly sagged against the wall, gulping her breath. He rose up and kissed her cheek in a gentlemanly fashion. Ryan the Rake, she thought.

She melted in spite of herself, in spite of the bad-boy boyishness that drew her to him, and touched the spot he'd kissed.

Swoon. Swoon. Swoon.

"Your turn," she told him, her voice floating, like the steam that surrounded them. She desperately wanted to give him the same type of pleasure.

She started at his neck, kissing and nibbling. She

worked her way down to his chest, his flat brown nipples, his navel.

Then lower...

His stomach muscles jumped as she tugged him closer. Down on her knees, she explored the masculine taste of him.

He recited her name, calling her "Tore," as she'd given him permission to do. He also groaned and shifted closer to the showerhead, making Victoria lean in the same direction so the water could splash her, too.

Elevating the waterfall fantasy to new heights.

Ryan and Victoria ate breakfast, then went into the woods to while away the rest of the morning. Now that their bellies were sated, along with their bodies, he couldn't think of anything else he would rather be doing.

As they sat on a blanket in a copse of trees, he said, "Do you think they're watching us now?"

"The nymphs?" She peered through their timbered shelter. "I don't know. Do you?"

"If they are, I hope they're enjoying this as much as I am." He stretched his legs out in front of him.

She said, "Wood nymphs aren't just mythical creatures. There's a butterfly by that name. And a hummingbird, too."

Fascinated, he sat forward. "So there could be *real* wood nymphs nearby?"

"The hummingbirds are from Central America. I think there is a species in Mexico, too. But there wouldn't be any in this area."

"What about the butterflies?"

"They inhabit the U.S."

"What do they look like?"

"They're brown with eyespots on their wings, but the number of spots varies from region to region. There would definitely be some around here."

"How do you know all of this?"

"I designed a website for an artist who paints woodland creatures, real and otherwise. It was a fun project, considering my love of woodland creatures, too."

"I liked the drawings you used to do."

"This artist is way better than I could ever be. Do you want to see her work?" She removed her phone and got online. "This is the site I designed for her. You can scroll through to see her paintings."

She handed him the phone, and he sat quietly and looked at the images. He took note of the site itself, too, and what a wonderful job Victoria had done. "It's beautiful. All of it. I'm going to keep my eye out for those butterflies. Wouldn't it be great if we saw one today?"

"They've probably flown past you a zillion times, but you never paid attention to them before."

He would be paying attention now. He took a good look around, but he didn't see anything except a grasshopper camouflaged amid the greenery. He shifted his focus to the phone. "What's your favorite work of hers?"

She leaned closer. "I like the fantasy ones the best." She enlarged a painting of a half-naked, strikingly beautiful nymph with long flowing hair and sparkling skin. "This is a depiction of Daphne. She's the daughter of the river god Peneus. She was also involved in a curse brought on by Eros, the god of love."

Ryan didn't know this story, as he'd never studied Greek mythology. "How so?"

"It starts with Apollo, the god of the sun, taunting

Eros and saying that he isn't as good with a bow and arrow as Apollo. Apollo is feeling full of himself because he just killed a gigantic snake. Eros decides to get back at Apollo and shoots him with an arrow that's tipped in gold and makes people fall in love. He also shoots Daphne with an arrow that's tipped in lead and does just the opposite. So while Apollo is falling in love with Daphne and chasing her around, she's appalled by his affection and is running away from him."

He thought about the gold dress Victoria had worn. Only she wasn't trying to make him fall in love. The symbolism wasn't the same.

"How does it turn out?" he asked.

"Daphne keeps running away from Apollo, but eventually he catches up to her. And just when he's about to grab her, she calls out to her father for help. Peneus comes to his daughter's aid by turning her into a laurel tree."

"Damn. What a dad. Remind me not to take lessons from him."

She smiled, laughed a little. "It's what Daphne wanted. She asked her father to change her form."

"And what about Apollo? How does he react?"

"He's grief-stricken that he lost his ladylove. He insists that he will never forget her. He wears a crown of laurel on his head and decorates his quiver and lyre with it. He also declares laurels as sacred, making them stay forever green."

"Then I guess it's a nice story, as long as Daphne is happy as a tree."

"Daphne never wanted to marry, anyway. Even before Apollo fell in love with her, she'd begged her father to allow her to remain a virgin."

"I wish laurels were indigenous to this area." Ryan wanted to get a glimpse of the independent Daphne.

"I think the closest thing would be an Oregon myrtle. In California they're called a California laurel. But I'm not sure if they're technically a laurel or a myrtle or either one. I'm not a tree expert."

"You know more than I do, and I'm the one who has always lived near the woods."

"I only know the trees that are associated with mythology. If you want a laurel tree, you can go to a nursery and get a bay laurel. You can grow it in a pot if you prefer not to get anything too big."

"Will you go with me? Today?" He definitely wanted one.

"Sure. Then I can make Italian food for dinner and spice the tomato sauce with some of its leaves."

"Anything that's going to result in another of your home-cooked meals is fine by me." Plus he was certain Daphne would approve of his choice to buy a laurel.

And the poor lovelorn Apollo, too.

After dinner, Ryan helped Victoria clean up. The pasta had tasted tremendous. The salad and garlic bread, too.

"I feel like I'm going to pop," he said.

"Me, too. We ate more than we should have." She handed him their plates so he could rinse them for the dishwasher.

While at the sink, he peered out the kitchen window at his new tree. It would always remind him of Victoria, and now he didn't know if that was good or bad.

Once again, he thought about her gold dress, likening it to Eros's gilded-tipped arrow, which he knew was foolish. Victoria wasn't out to get him.

"I'm a little confused," he said.

"About what?"

"Eros. You said he was the god of love. But I always thought that's who Cupid was."

"Cupid is from Roman mythology and Eros is Greek. But they're the same type of god."

"So basically, they're both little troublemakers?"

She walked away to wipe down the counters. "I suppose you could say that."

"Who are the gods of sex and desire?"

"There are lots of them, but Cupid and Eros would still be in those categories, too."

Ryan dried his hands and came up behind her. "Then in that case, Cupid and Eros are working their voodoo on me, with the sex and desire part, anyway. I can't seem to stop wanting you." He leaned over her shoulder and inhaled the vanilla fragrance on her skin. She was wearing it again today.

"I can't stop wanting you, either." She turned around, putting them face to face. "You have no idea what it's been like for me. I worked so hard to not want you, yet here I am, having this affair."

"Then go ahead and blame it on Eros or Cupid or whoever."

"Rather than take responsibility for my own actions? That probably isn't the wisest choice."

"No, but it's easier." He lowered his head to kiss her.

She didn't protest. She looped her arms around him, and their mouths met in lusty abandonment.

Until the sound of the front door opening jarred them apart, alerting them that Kaley was home.

Victoria hastily righted her appearance. "Do you think she saw us?"

"No." The kitchen wasn't visible from the entryway. "But I think she's headed this way."

"Then don't just stand there." She went back to wiping down the counters. "Do something. Look busy."

He resumed his spot at the sink, turned on the water and blasted the spaghetti pot.

Kaley soon entered the kitchen. "I thought I heard you guys in here."

"Oh, hi honey." Victoria sounded a bit too chipper, like a fifties-sitcom mom. "We didn't know you were home." If she were Pinocchio, her nose would've grown by a mile.

But who was Ryan to judge her? He was guilty of the same lie. "You sneaked up on us, kiddo," he added for good measure, even though he'd never called her kiddo before.

Victoria rushed over to the fridge. "Are you hungry? There are plenty of leftovers."

"That's okay. I already ate." The teenager angled her head. "Are you guys okay? You're acting weird."

Acting was exactly what they were doing. And badly, Ryan thought. No one would be passing out Academy Awards at this misguided event.

"We're fine," Victoria said.

"Totally fine," he parroted.

Kaley squinted. "You seem like you just had a fight or something."

Ryan shifted his feet. They hadn't been fighting anything but desire.

Victoria said, "We had a nice dinner, and when you

came in we were doing the dishes and cleaning up. Ryan even got a new tree today."

Kaley made a perplexed expression. "Aren't there enough of those around here? Like in the woods?"

Victoria explained. "It's a bay tree. I used some of its leaves to season our food."

"Can't you get bay leaves in the spice department at the market? Did Ryan have to buy a whole tree for that?"

He jumped into the conversation, trying to clarify the confusion, if he could. "I didn't buy it for tonight's meal. I bought it because Victoria told me a story that inspired me."

Kaley still seem perplexed. "What kind of story makes someone want to buy a tree?"

"It was about Apollo and Daphne."

"Oh." The teenager got it, thank goodness. "Daphne was the chick who got turned into a tree." She sought Ryan's gaze. "That's nice that it inspired you."

"Thanks," he replied, praying that was the last of it.

Luckily, it was. Kaley changed the subject. "Guess what June and I uncovered in our research?" She answered her own question. "Some of the information we were looking for about your mom."

Surprised and interested, Ryan went into the living room with Kaley to discuss her findings. Victoria came along, too.

Their daughter said, "Molly's name was on an ancestry site. Margaret Mary Dodd. I knew it was her because your dad was on the same site and was listed as her husband."

"Then it's definitely her. What else did it say?"

"That her mother's name was Georgia May Dodd

and that her father was unknown. I assume that means that his name wasn't on her birth certificate. Oh, and get this—Georgia had Molly when she was seventeen. She was a teenage mother."

Ryan glanced at Victoria to catch her reaction and saw that she was looking at him, too, obviously affected by the connection.

Kaley continued. "But Georgia died when she was eighteen, only a year after Molly was born."

"Oh, that's sad," Victoria said.

Kaley nodded. "It made me feel bad, too. But it also explains why Ryan's dad said that Molly had been raised by an elderly aunt."

"How did Georgia die?" he asked, curious about his young, tragic grandmother.

"I don't know. The ancestry site only had the year she was born and the year she died. The cause of death wasn't included."

"Did you find out which Paiute band my mom is registered with?"

"According to the National Archives, she was Southern Paiute and she was registered with a Utah band."

"Utah?" He would have guessed that his mom was Northern Paiute and was registered with an Oregon band, which proved how little he knew about her or himself, for that matter.

"You can register with them, too," Kaley said. "But you'll have to contact the tribal office to see what kind of paperwork they'll need from you."

Most likely the same paperwork his father had given to the adoption agency, he thought. "Was there anything in your research that indicated that my mother or grandmother ever lived in Utah?"

"No. But not everyone lives near their tribe or on a reservation or in Indian country. My dad is from the Cherokee Nation of Oklahoma and he's never been to Oklahoma."

"Yes, but your dad was still raised within his culture. I've never had anything to do with mine." Nor had he considered researching his lineage. He'd just accepted his ignorance. "I've never even been to a powwow."

"Oh, my God, seriously?" His daughter sounded shocked. "Even Victoria has been to one."

He turned to his secret lover. "You have?"

She nodded. "I attended a gathering about a year ago."

Curious, he studied her. "Why?"

"Because it was around the time I started thinking about searching for Kaley, and I was trying to feel closer to her, to the Native child I'd birthed. I walked around, looking at all the girls who were around her age at the time, wondering if any of them could be her."

"That's nice. Really nice." But as usual, Ryan felt completely out of the loop when it came to these types of matters. "So when and where do most powwows take place?"

Kaley replied, "They take place all over, reservations, fairgrounds, schools, parks." She bopped up. "Do you want me to check my computer and see if there are any going on in this part of Oregon over the next weekend?"

Ryan's pulse skittered. "Yes, absolutely." He wanted to attend a Native gathering, to try to bond with his heritage. But more importantly, he wanted Victoria and Kaley by his side.

* * *

On Sunday afternoon, Ryan sat on a lawn chair, in between Victoria and Kaley, immersed in his very first intertribal powwow. The sun peeked through the clouds, the drum pounded like a heartbeat and the dancers twirled in the arena.

The drum was composed of the instrument itself, as well as the singers, and was regarded with utmost respect. Kaley had told him to think of it like a grandparent. So while he listened to the songs, he thought of his grandmother. He thought about his mother, too, and wondered if she and Georgia were watching from above.

He glanced over at Kaley, and she smiled. Next he looked at Victoria, and she smiled, too. He couldn't have asked for a more beautiful feeling.

While they watched the dancers, Kaley said, "In the old days, the war dance was either a prelude to war or used in celebration when the warriors returned from battle."

Ryan was being educated by his daughter, enjoying the young, spirited sound of her voice.

She continued by saying, "The men's fancy dance is loosely based on the war dance. It's also called the fancy feather or fancy war dance. The Paiute call it the fancy bustle." She motioned with the tilt of her head, gesturing to a group of male dancers who were wearing two large bustles of brightly colored feathers. She hadn't pointed to them because traditional Indians weren't supposed to point. She'd been teaching Ryan all sorts of traditional things.

"Fancy anything is a good name for it." The speed, agility and flamboyant footwork dazzled the eye. It was his favorite dance, the most entertaining by far. "But I like fancy bustle the best."

"Because that's what your tribe calls it? I'll bet there are lots of Paiute here." She grinned. "Including us."

Us. Him and her. He returned her cheeky grin. She'd been raised Cherokee, but her Paiute blood came from him.

"I used to dance a lot when I was little," she said as a tot shuffled by, clutching an older child's hand. "I don't dance that much anymore. But I definitely want to teach my kids to be part of the circle."

Ryan wondered what it would be like to raise a child in this environment. Of course he didn't know anything about raising a child in *any* environment. He was only learning to be a dad, eighteen years after the fact.

"If this was my heritage, I would dance," Victoria said.

"You still can," Kaley told her. "In the dances that are open to everyone."

Ryan smiled at Victoria. "I can see you out there, dressed in your finery."

The women's clothing, which ranged from buckskin to taffeta, included colorful accessories, items such as fringed shawls, beaded fans and ornamental moccasins. He imagined her draped in gold.

"I can see you out there, too," she replied. "I can see powwows becoming part of your world."

He appreciated her confidence. "Maybe someday I'll learn to dance."

"You're already a good dancer." She spoke quietly now, out of their daughter's earshot.

"Thanks." He spoke softly, too. He knew she was

referring to the night they'd danced on the patio. "So are you."

They both fell silent, lost in the twinkling-light memory.

Soon Kaley interrupted the quiet and suggested they get some fry bread. "You have to try it," she told Ryan.

He'd seen plenty of people indulging in the fried discs, either smothered in taco fixings or dusted with powdered sugar. "Sure. I'm game."

"Good thing." She joked, "'Cause you'll never be a proper Indian until you stuff your face with fry bread."

He chuckled. "Then by all means, make me a proper Indian."

The three of them got up and headed toward the food stands, searching for the shortest line.

Kaley and Ryan ordered the taco variety, and Victoria went for a plain one, sweetening it herself with a complimentary shaker of powdered sugar.

Rather than return to their lawn chairs, they occupied a picnic bench. Kaley watched Ryan take the first bite. He nodded, flashed a thumbs-up sign and kept eating. It was beyond delicious.

"Do you think he looks any different to you?" Kaley asked Victoria, continuing the transformation joke.

"I don't know." She sized him up. "I think he's the same as before."

He swallowed the food in his mouth. "Handsome as ever, right?"

Both females laughed.

"He's always so conceited," Kaley said. "But we love him, anyway."

Ryan nearly choked, quite happily, on his next bite. His daughter had just said that she loved him, teasingly, but she'd still said it. He loved her, too, not teasingly, but for real. She'd carved out a special place in his heart.

Overwhelmed, he glanced over at Victoria. She appeared to be ignoring Kaley's admission, making sure that Ryan didn't get the impression that she was willingly part of the "we" Kaley had referred to. But he already knew that she wasn't.

Still, it bugged him that she was trying so hard to make her point. Couldn't she behave with a just bit of that twinkling-light tenderness from before?

Instead, she kept her gaze averted from his. Would he feel better if he reached over and took her hand, if he skimmed his lips across her knuckles, if he "outed" their affair? Maybe. But he didn't do it.

Determined to keep his wits, he focused on his Indian taco, on his Indian daughter, on the reason he was here.

"Ready?" Kaley said, after they finished eating.

"For what?" he asked.

"To walk around and check out the crafts."

"Only if you let me buy you a gift, and I want it to be something special, something substantial." He didn't want her going home with a cheap trinket.

Kaley grinned. "Are you kidding? I love getting free stuff."

"What about you?" he asked Victoria. "Will you let me buy you something, too?" In a sense, he was challenging her. Trying to force her to accept a token associated with the day Kaley had included her in loving Ryan, even if it wasn't true.

Before Victoria could refuse, Kaley said, "Traditional Indians think it's rude to turn down a gift."

Perfect, Ryan thought. Now Victoria was stuck.

She adhered to protocol. "Then of course I'll accept a gift. I wouldn't want to defy tradition."

"It has to be substantial, like Kaley's present. A good piece of jewelry or a nice basket."

"Take the jewelry," their daughter said in typical girl fashion.

Victoria conservatively replied, "I'd rather have a basket."

Ryan said, "Okay." But a few minutes later, when he thought about how impersonal a basket was, he wished he would have insisted on jewelry.

They browsed the booths. Kaley had fun shopping for her gift. She went for a stunning bracelet that fit her style. She also wanted a novelty item, a pendant that had "Proud to be Paiute" written on it. Ryan couldn't imagine anything sweeter. His daughter was a gem.

Victoria's shopping expedition was much more reserved, as expected. Ryan suggested that she get a Paiute-made basket, trying to make it a bit more personal.

So they went from booth to booth until they found a vendor who carried quality Paiute goods. Each flat round basket in the collection looked similar, with almost the same design. Ryan was disappointed that there wasn't a bigger variety. Victoria chose one quickly, without much fanfare. Even Kaley wandered off to look at something else.

While Ryan was in the process of paying for the item, the vendor volunteered its origin.

The man said, "Did you know that when Paiute women started selling their baskets, their main customer was the Navajo?"

That seemed to intrigue Victoria. Finally a spark of

interest. She moved closer to the counter and asked, "Why did the Navajo buy baskets from the Paiute?"

"Because a traditional Navajo wedding ceremony involves the bride and groom feeding each other corn-meal from this style of basket, and the Paiute make such beautiful—"

"That's a wedding basket?" Victoria's cheeks flushed.

"Yes, my dear, it is."

As the man turned away to wrap it, she stood like a statue. For a moment Ryan did, too. He'd warned her not to rush into becoming a bride, and now he was giv-ing her an object that symbolized marriage. He never would have done that purposely. But it was too late to buy her something else, not without calling more at-tention to the discomfort that had already been incited.

Ryan considered saying that he was sorry for forcing her to accept a gift from him, but that would probably make it worse. Besides, wedding baskets were obviously an important part of Paiute history, which also meant they were part of his ancestry.

And in that sense, he wanted her to have it.

Chapter Eleven

On Monday morning Victoria and Kaley accompanied Ryan to work. After they met his staff, who graced them with bright smiles and tons of enthusiasm, they spent a little time hanging around the clinic, fussing over his furry patients.

And now Kaley was off with June somewhere, and Victoria was alone in her room, trying to concentrate on her work.

Fat chance.

She glanced at the clock on her laptop. Ryan would be arriving at her door soon. He'd promised to come see her on his lunch hour, not to indulge in food but to…

Kiss, she thought. Touch. Make love.

They hadn't had sex since the day after their prom. Of course Victoria had more on her mind than entertaining him this afternoon. She was also stressing about the wedding basket.

She'd wanted so badly to marry Ryan when she was younger, and now she was stuck with an item she would have died over back then. He hadn't been thrilled about the basket at first, either, but he'd warmed up to it, even showing it to Kaley and discussing the design. But neither he nor their daughter knew how truly awful it was for her, particularly since Ryan had married someone else.

A knock sounded on the door, and she jumped up and smoothed her summer skirt, preparing for her rendezvous.

She answered the summons, invited him into her room and locked the door behind them. He wore his lab coat, looking deliciously doctorly.

Did his ex, the veterinarian he'd married, look good in her lab coat, too? Was she as pretty as she was smart?

If Victoria was smart, she would end this right now. But apparently she wasn't very bright. With the fierceness of a woman scorned, she grabbed Ryan and kissed him, using her pain as passion.

Aroused by her quick come-on, he returned her forceful kiss and backed her against the wall. Strong and rough, he pulled her girlie T-shirt over her head and exposed her lace-trimmed bra.

Not to be outdone, she yanked his shirt free of his trousers and opened his fly, rubbing him until he groaned and cupped her rear.

She impatiently asked, "Did you bring protection?"

He was still clutching her butt. "The necessary nuisance? It's in my pocket."

She fished out the condom, ordering him to use it. He gave her an order, too, telling her to ditch her panties.

They moved like lightning. Within the pulse of five

or six frantic heartbeats, her panties were gone, her skirt was hiked past her hips, and he was sheathed in latex and thrusting inside her. He feasted on her lips, too, nipping and biting.

They made sinfully fast love, neither caring how quickly the climax came. If anything, it seemed to be a deliberate race to the feral finish line.

They found it together, at the very same time, with a prism of colors exploding before Victoria's eyes.

When her vision cleared, when she could breathe without gasping, she got dressed, putting her T-shirt and panties back in place.

He adjusted his clothes, too, after he discarded the necessary nuisance.

Now that there was no evidence of what they'd done, besides her pink-tinged skin, he hauled her back into his arms and planted another power-packed kiss on her sore-from-sex lips.

"You don't play fair," she said, trying to keep from wobbling under his touch.

He released her. "You started it."

"How much time do you have before you have to go back to work?"

"Enough time to hang out and talk if you want."

"About what?"

"I don't know." He combed a hand through his hair. "Anything."

Was he offering to talk as a form of afterglow? She appreciated the sentiment, strange as it seemed in this situation. But the only thing she could think to say as he stood there in his crisp lab coat with his trousers properly zipped was, "Your staff was really nice. I'm glad I got to meet them."

"They thought you and Kaley were wonderful, too. Betty kept singing both of your praises."

Betty was the tech whose kids made ice cream from Mabel's milk. "Oh, that's sweet."

"She asked me if I was bringing the two of you to the mixer tonight, but I told her that I wasn't going."

"What mixer?"

"It's a chamber of commerce thing."

Did that mean that his ex might be in attendance? Naturally, Victoria couldn't help but wonder. "Were you planning on going before Kaley and I decided to stay the extra week?"

"Yes, but—"

"You should go and take us."

"It would be boring for you."

"No, it wouldn't. I want to go. And I'll bet Kaley will, too, if she can bring June along."

"Jackie and Don will probably be there, Victoria. She normally attends these sorts of events."

She played it down. "I don't mind meeting her if you don't mind making the introduction."

"Sure, okay, why not? It's not as if your being here is a secret. Besides, I'd like for her to see how beautiful and grown-up our daughter is. And how gorgeous and sophisticated you are, too."

All right, then. She fluttered with anxious excitement, eager to make the other woman's acquaintance.

And to put Ryan's married past behind her once and for all.

When evening rolled around, Victoria stood in front of the closet door mirror in her room, putting the finishing touches on her appearance. Ryan sat on the edge of her bed, watching her and making her self-conscious.

"You shouldn't be in my room," she said.

"Don't worry. Kaley isn't going to catch me in here. You know as well as I do that she isn't home."

Yes, she knew. Kaley and June had gone out to dinner with some of June's other friends. Later, the entire group was going to meet up with Ryan and Victoria at the mixer. "You still shouldn't be in here."

"Why? Because I'm making you nervous? You're primping like we're going to another prom."

She spun around to glare at him. She'd donned a little black dress and spiced it up with her new gold heels. "Would you prefer I show up in a pair of holey jeans?"

"Don't get testy. I'm not complaining. You look absolutely amazing. But I'm not naive. I know the only reason you want to go to this mixer is to check Jackie out."

"Can you blame me?"

"No, but you're not in competition with her."

"If that wasn't an issue, then you wouldn't have said what you'd said earlier. How you want Jackie to see how beautiful and grown-up our daughter is. And how gorgeous and sophisticated I am."

"Yes, but it wasn't my idea to bring you and Kaley. I didn't arrange for it to happen this way. I'm not deliberately trying to show you off to my ex."

"But when the opportunity arose, you took it."

He stole her line. "Can you blame me?"

Touché, she thought. "Did you ever consider ending your association with the chamber?"

"You mean after the divorce? No."

"Why not?"

"Because networking with friends and business associates is part of who I am, and life doesn't stop at divorce."

"It must have been difficult at first, knowing that you were going to run into Jackie at the meetings."

"It would have been easier not to see her. Particularly when I was alone and she was cozied up to Don. But I'm used to that now."

"Being alone or her being with Don?"

"Both. But at the moment, I'm not alone. You're here with me."

She thought about the restaurant owner who'd treated them like royalty. "Is Isa going to be at this mixer?"

"Probably. He's on the board of directors."

"What if he acts like we're a couple in front of Kaley?"

"So what if he does? People at the barbecue did that, too. Besides, we didn't kiss in front of Isa or do anything that marked us as couple. All we did in his presence was have dinner."

"Before you booked the reservation, you told him that you were taking your old girlfriend on a fancy reunion date. That screams romance."

"It does not."

"It does, too."

"If you're going to stress about tonight, then let's not go. I can call Kaley and tell her that we're canceling."

"No." The word leaped like a frog from her throat. She was already geared up to meet Jackie. To cancel now would leave her with an unresolved feeling. "It will be fine. Like you said before, people already know that Kaley and I are visiting you. None of this is a secret."

"None of it except our affair."

She turned back to the mirror and started fussing

with her appearance again, catching Ryan's reflection in the mirror. Would Jackie figure out that they were having an affair?

Probably, she thought. Women, especially former wives, had that kind of radar. Or so she assumed. Victoria wasn't an authority on being a wife.

Former or otherwise.

The mixer was being held at a new pawnshop that had opened in town. At first Victoria thought that it seemed like an unlikely setting for a cocktails and hors d'oeuvres party, but it worked out well. There was plenty of room to mill about and lots of interesting items to look at. Plus in this economic climate, pawnshops were all the rage.

The guests were an eclectic mixture of young, old and in between. Kaley and her friends hadn't arrived yet, but Victoria expected them to be late. Jackie and Don hadn't made an appearance yet, either. Not that she would recognize them on sight. She had no idea what either of them looked like. She only knew they weren't here because Ryan said they weren't.

He glanced over at her and smiled, sending her heart into a tailspin. He was chatting with the owner of a sporting goods store. She could see why Ryan enjoyed these events. This was his town, his element, his world.

Suddenly Victoria wanted to run back to California as fast as her sexy gold pumps would take her. She knew better than to get close to Ryan, but she'd done it anyway, foolishly convincing herself that she could handle it. But clearly, she couldn't. Why else would she want to meet his ex-wife? Victoria wasn't healing from the past. She was mired in it, particularly since she was still wondering if Jackie would be able to detect their affair.

Needing to move around the room, she wandered over to a display case, curious to see what was in it.

Seriously? Was there no escape? The dang thing was filled with wedding rings. First a wedding basket and now this? Talk about a comedy of errors. Only she wasn't laughing.

Nor did she walk away. She actually inched closer, spotting an engagement ring with a pear-shaped diamond that she liked. Naturally, she wondered why it was being pawned. Was it the product of divorce? Death? Or was the couple still married and facing financial problems? Whatever the scenario, she shouldn't be concerned about it. That ring wasn't going to end up on her finger.

"Victoria?" Ryan said her name from behind her. She recognized his voice.

She turned around, hoping that he didn't notice the contents in the display case. He didn't appear to. His thoughts seemed elsewhere.

"They're here," he said.

She took a deep breath. His thoughts were definitely elsewhere. She asked, "Jackie and Don?"

He nodded. "Do you want me to introduce you now or after the girls get here?"

"Now." She didn't want to wait. That would only make her more nervous. "You can introduce Kaley to her later."

"Okay. Then let's do this." He led her toward a couple who stood near the hors d'oeuvres table.

"Is that them?" she asked, making sure.

"Yes."

Victoria took note of their appearances. Jackie was an attractive brunette, about medium height, in a flowing beige dress and strappy sandals. She wore her hair neat and stylish and her makeup soft and breezy. Don was older than Victoria expected, late-forties or so, and already graying at the temples. He had the look of a man who spent his days outdoors.

Jackie glanced up from her drink. Don looked up, too, and put his arm lightly around his fiancée's waist.

As Victoria got closer, she noticed that Jackie's eyes were a pale shade of blue. She was also wearing an engagement ring as dazzling as the one Victoria had been admiring.

Had Ryan given her a ring like that, too? And if he had, what had Jackie done with it after the divorce?

Ryan made the introductions, and the four of them engaged in small talk until the men were approached by another guest. That left Victoria and Jackie to fend for themselves, but being alone actually made things easier.

Jackie said, "When Ryan and I first got together, he confided in me about what happened at the hospital." She spoke in a hushed tone. "I always felt bad for you."

"I know. He told me that you were sympathetic toward me." There was no point in pretending that this wasn't what it was. "I felt bad for you, too, once he explained why your marriage ended."

"None of that is important now." Jackie glanced lovingly at Don. "I'm with the man I'm supposed to be with."

"I'm glad for you."

The other woman angled her head, looking closely at Victoria. The ex-wife radar?

Then she said, "Thank you, that's nice of you. I'm

glad that Ryan got to meet his daughter. I heard that she's in town, too."

"She'll be here later. We'll be sure to introduce you."

"Oh, that would be nice. I'd like to meet her. Don and I are going to work on having a family soon after we're married. I don't want to wait."

"I'm sure you'll make a terrific mom."

"And Don will be a terrific father."

Victoria imagined the birth being just as it should be, happy and loving—and so unlike what she'd experienced.

"This is good that we're meeting and talking like this," Jackie said. "It brings closure."

"I think so, too." Only she wasn't feeling quite the same sense of closure, not with the fear that she was getting too close to Ryan.

The men drifted back over to the women, and Jackie and Don excused themselves to mingle. Ryan didn't ask Victoria her opinion of Jackie.

But she told him anyway by saying, "She was very nice." She softly added, "We had a meaningful discussion."

"Don and I have never had a meaningful discussion. Men don't normally do that." He paused, met her gaze. "And just for the record, you're nice, too. One of the nicest people I know. I'm honored to be here with you tonight."

Her heart gave a little twirl, and she wished that she could kiss him in this very public place. More proof of how her feelings for him were escalating.

He stayed by her side for the rest of the party, and when Kaley arrived, they reunited with Jackie and Don to make the introduction.

On the surface it seemed to go well. Kaley was friendly and polite, and Jackie marveled at how much their daughter favored Ryan.

But even so, Victoria noticed that Kaley seemed out of sorts. Soon after meeting Jackie, the teenager wandered off with her friends, keeping a distance from her parents, but still glancing over at Victoria every so often, when she thought Victoria wasn't looking.

Once they got home, Victoria took matters into her own hands. Ryan hadn't noticed that Kaley seemed off, so she didn't alert him to the problem. She waited until he went to bed to go to Kaley's room and talk to her.

They sat quietly, both dressed in their pajamas.

Victoria said, "Tell me what's going on, honey. Tell me what was bothering you tonight."

"How could you tell that something was wrong?"

"I noticed the way you were looking at me."

"It's because of how strange you and Ryan have been acting. I even talked to June about it, and she's been trying to help me figure it out. I noticed that it started on the day Ryan bought the tree, and it's been weird ever since. Sometimes you guys seem okay, and sometimes you don't."

Victoria sighed. The tree day was when they'd almost gotten caught kissing in the kitchen. "We've been dealing with some things."

"Does it have anything to do with Jackie? Because June and I thought it was strange that you wanted to meet her."

"Jackie isn't the problem."

"Then what is?"

At this point, she owed Kaley the truth. But she took

a moment to think about how to phrase it. "Ryan and I got caught up in the past and we're involved again. But only while I'm here. After I go home, it's going to end."

"We actually wondered if it was something like that. Except for…"

"Except for what?"

"It still seems like maybe Jackie…" Kaley let her statement drift again.

"Just say it, honey, say what you're thinking."

"That maybe Jackie is part of the problem. Not because she still cares about Ryan or anything, but because she used to be his wife and you were the girl he left at the hospital."

Her daughter was dangerously close to hitting the mark. "I'm not jealous of Jackie. That wasn't what I was experiencing tonight. I actually liked her very much. My problem is that I'm confused about my feelings for Ryan."

"Because you like him too much or not enough?"

"Too much." She went ahead and admitted the rest of it. "I used to love him when I was young. I never told him, though. I never told anyone." Victoria fussed with a loose thread on her nightgown. "He still doesn't know. Not about how I felt in the past or about how I how feel now. The closer we get, the more fearful I am that I might fall in love with him again."

"It isn't good to keep secrets like that, Victoria."

"No, it isn't. But it's easier for me to keep it to myself. I don't see a future with Ryan, and I'd rather not love him."

"I think it would be great if you got together for real."

Her heart bounced off her chest. "You'd want us to be a couple?"

"Of course. You're my birth parents. Why wouldn't I want for you to make it work?"

"That's nice, but like I said, I'd rather not love him."

"'Cause it hurt too much last time?"

"Yes." She considered her daughter and how mature she seemed, discussing this like an adult. "Maybe I should tell him how I feel." Maybe it was time for the secrets to end.

"I agree that you should tell him." The teenager frowned. "How come you guys hid your romance from me? How come when I noticed that both of you were acting strange, like that day in the kitchen, you didn't just admit what was going on?"

"That was my choice, not Ryan's. I figured our affair was going to end so quickly, it didn't bear mentioning. Plus I didn't want to set a bad example for you."

"A bad example? That's goofy."

"It is not."

"It is, too. I mean, come on, it's not as if I'm a virgin or anything. And even if I was, I wouldn't go off and get laid just because you guys are doing it."

Stunned, Victoria merely stared. She had no idea that Kaley had already been sexually active. "Who were you with?"

"My old boyfriend."

"Did you love him?"

"No. But I liked him."

"You shouldn't do it again until you love someone."

"Says the voice of experience? You're not exactly the poster child for abstinence."

"Now do you see what I mean about setting a bad example?"

"Yes, but doing it and not telling me about it is hypocritical."

Damn this generation. They were too smart for their own good. "Just think about what I said, okay? Sex is always better when you love someone."

"Then maybe you should start loving Ryan again or stop sleeping with him."

"Ha. Ha. Ms. Funny."

Kaley laughed. "Sorry." She paused, turned serious. "I actually think you should move into Ryan's room for the rest of the days that we're here."

"You do? Why?"

"Because I'd rather see you acting like normal parents instead of being sneaky and weird."

Ah, yes, the normalcy thing. Only no matter how you sliced it, none of this was normal. Still, Victoria agreed that it was a better option than keeping secrets. "I'll discuss everything with Ryan."

"When?"

"Tonight." Even if it meant waking him up. She needed to do it before she lost her nerve. She needed to come clean—about the past and the present.

No matter how difficult the truth was.

Chapter Twelve

The last thing Ryan expected was for Victoria to enter his room. He hadn't fallen asleep yet, but he was half-naked and shrouded in darkness.

"I need to talk to you," she said. "Can I turn on the light?"

He would've preferred to leave the lights off and pull her under the covers with him. But this obviously wasn't a booty call, not with her saying that she needed to talk, and not with Kaley just down the hall.

"Sure. Go ahead." He gave her permission to brighten the room.

She went full bore, flipping the main switch instead of a softer nightlight. He squinted from the invasion. By now he was sitting up in bed.

Victoria stood beside the door, looking like an angel in a simple white nightgown. He could see the faint outline of her panties beneath it. They were white, as well.

She moved closer. She seemed nervous. He was getting a little nervous, too. He suspected that this talk wasn't going to be pleasant, no matter how ethereal she looked.

"Kaley knows about us," she said.

He blew out a breath. "Is she mad?"

"No. She thinks that I should start sleeping in here with you for the remainder of our visit. To her that would make you and I seem more like normal parents. She doesn't like the idea of us sneaking around."

Ryan mentally thanked their daughter. This conversation wasn't the least bit unpleasant. "I didn't like sneaking around, either."

"I know. And you were right about that. We should have been up front with Kaley from the start."

He patted the space next to him. "No harm, no foul. Now that it's settled, you can get into bed with me and we can get some sleep."

She didn't advance forward. "I'm not done yet. There are things I need to say. Things I've been dealing with."

He should have known it couldn't be that simple. "Then go on. Say your piece."

A deep breath. A hesitation.

"Come on, Victoria. Just do it."

"Okay. Here's the first part—I used to be in love with you, Ryan."

If the bed had opened up and swallowed him whole, he wouldn't have been more surprised. Or more rattled. He didn't know how to respond.

Finally after a heart-pounding silence, he asked, "What's the second part?"

"My healing isn't going as well as it seems. And if I don't get a handle on it, I'm afraid I could fall in love with you again. But I'm trying not to let that happen. I don't want to feel that way. When I leave here, I want to be free of those types of emotions."

He thought about her gold dress, about Eros's gold-tipped arrow, about how much he was going to miss her when she was gone. He thought about everything that was jumbled inside his head, including his fear that she might be with Eric someday.

Should he tell her how he felt, should he relay his fears? Yes, he should. But he couldn't seem to do it, especially the Eric part. But on the other hand, he couldn't sit here and encourage her to love him, either. He was still reeling from the confusion, unsure of what was expected of him.

He made a silly joke. His way of coping. "Should I start acting like a jerk so you don't cave in and love me?"

"That's not funny." But she smiled, anyway.

"Sometimes comic relief helps."

"I agree. Sometimes it does."

"It is helping now?"

"Yes." She inched closer to the bed and sat on the edge of it. "But I can't make light of how painful it was to love you when we were younger. I wanted to marry you, Ryan."

Her words kicked him square in the gut, making his muscles tense, making him flinch. How could he have been so blind to her feelings? "I'm sorry. I had no idea."

"It was dumb of me to want that. It never would have worked. But I dreamed of it, anyway."

"You must really hate that wedding basket."

"Are you making another joke?"

"No, Tore. I'm being serious this time."

"Then you're right, in a sense I do hate it. And I hate that you married Jackie, even though there's nothing between you anymore."

She still looked like an angel, white and pure, which made him seem darker. Not just his skin and his hair, but his aura. He said, "I understand why you're being cautious."

She went silent.

"I want you to heal, Victoria. I want to you to be free of the pain." Pain that went far deeper than he'd ever realized. To think that she'd loved him enough to want to marry him. That she'd dreamed of being his wife. It boggled his mind.

She sighed. "I actually do feel a little better now that I got it off my chest."

"That's good." That was how it should be. Except that Ryan was beginning to feel considerably worse. Only he didn't know if it was ego or his heart that was taking the hit. He prayed that it wasn't his heart. He couldn't bear to love her, not if she couldn't bear to love him.

"Do you want to come to bed now?" he asked. In spite of his mixed-up feelings, he had the urge to hold her.

"I'm still too wired to sleep."

"I meant to cuddle."

"Oh, that's nice. I'd like that."

She turned out the light and got under the covers. She curled up next to him, resting her head in the crook of his arm.

"This was such an overwhelming day," she said.

"For me, too." And it was still affecting him, turning his existence up and down and all around. Emotional vertigo, he thought. He'd never experienced anything quite like it. No, that wasn't true. He'd felt this way after he'd left her alone at the hospital. "Why didn't you tell me that you loved me when we were young?"

"I was scared to say something like that. Plus I kept hoping I would see signs that you loved me, too."

"What kind of signs?"

"The kind teenage girls manifest in their minds."

He pressed her for a definitive answer. "Like what, exactly?"

"Like you talking about a future between us. Or you giving me a promise ring like some of the other boys gave their girlfriends."

"I wonder how many of those promise-ring couples are still together."

"I don't know. But some people actually marry their high school sweethearts." She shifted in his arms. "You know what's weird? I was looking at wedding rings earlier. At the pawnshop," she explained. "It wasn't intentional, though."

"You just walked up to a display case and there they were?"

"Pretty much. In fact, it's what I was looking at when you came up to me and told me that Jackie and Don were there. But I could tell that you weren't aware of what was in the case."

"I offered to buy you jewelry at the powwow."

"What would you have done if I'd chosen a ring at the powwow?"

His pulse spiked. "Is that what you would have picked?"

"No. But I'm just asking, what would you have done if it that *had* been my choice?"

"I would have bought it for you."

"What if it had been an engagement-type ring?"

His pulse spiked even higher. "Did they have those types of rings at the powwow?"

"I noticed a few when Kaley was shopping for her bracelet."

He hadn't noticed them. "What were they like?"

"They were contemporary pieces with turquoise and diamonds mixed together."

"Sounds interesting."

"They were. Interesting. Unique. Beautiful."

"For someone who isn't on the deliberate lookout for a ring, you certainly have your eyes peeled for them."

"I do not."

"Yes, you do."

When she started to pull away from him, he tugged her back into his arms. "I didn't mean that in a bad way, Tore."

"Then how did you mean it?"

"I think it's only natural that you notice rings, especially when you're hanging out with the guy you wanted to marry. In that regard, it makes sense that you chose a wedding basket for your gift, too, even if you didn't know that's what you were choosing."

"Why? Because it was the universe's way of making me face my demons? You insisted that I buy something, and you're the one who suggested a Paiute basket."

"Then maybe the universe was sending me a message, too, a message that led to us having this discussion."

She quietly said, "I have to admit, there was an engagement ring at the pawnshop that I liked. The origins of where it might have come from bothered me, though. It also made me wonder what Jackie did with the ring you gave her."

"Actually, she gave it back to me while we were going through the divorce. I told her to keep it, but she didn't want it."

"So what did you do with it?"

"I sold it, along with my wedding band, and gave the money to an adoption foundation."

"An animal adoption foundation?"

"No. One for children. I've donated to them before." His way of helping a cause that had impacted his life.

"That's nice." She drew an imaginary line on his arm, as if she were tattooing him with an invisible design. It felt like a heart with a bunch of swirls, but he couldn't be sure. Nor did he want to speculate too deeply.

"So, Ryan, what would you have done if I would have admitted that I loved you and that I wanted to keep our baby and marry you?"

He wished that he could sweep her back in time and give her a romantic answer, but they both knew that wasn't possible. "I honestly don't know. But considering how I panicked when Kaley was born, it's probably better that you didn't tell me."

"I'm glad we're talking about it now."

So was he, for her sake, anyway. For him, it only complicated his already-complicated feelings. He was afraid of letting her go at the end of the week, just as he was afraid of wanting to keep her.

She rolled over on top of him, and his heart slammed his chest.

"What are you doing?" he asked. His voice came out raw.

"What does it feel like I'm doing?"

She ran her hand along the waistband of his shorts, arousing him, making him pray for redemption. He hadn't been expecting her to seduce him tonight. But maybe it was part of her cleansing and the demons she was trying to banish.

She stripped him bare, and the breath in his lungs whooshed out. Victoria was good at using sex to combat her feelings.

"I'm not going to let it happen," she said.

He knew that *it* was a euphemism for love. Her way of telling him that no matter how beautifully or wildly they made love, she wasn't going to repeat her sin from the past and fall in love with him again.

He understood. By God, he did. He couldn't bear to think of how badly she'd been hurt by the boy she'd once loved. He wanted to keep her from ever getting hurt again.

She turned on the bedside lamp and opened the nightstand drawer, obviously looking for protection.

After securing a packet, she tore it open. While she put the condom on him, he watched her: the determination on her face, the way she was intent on taking charge.

She peeled off her nightgown and removed her panties, and he watched her do that, too, the amber glow from the lamp bathing her skin.

Once she straddled him, he raised up to kiss her, to hold her, to keep her protectively close. Together, they rocked back and forth, their bodies undulating. She tunneled her hands through his hair; he gripped her waist and heightened the motion. They kept moving, bound in heat, locked in a soul-clenching, heart-thumping dance.

That wasn't allowed to be love.

* * *

While Ryan was at work, Victoria moved her belongings into his room. Kaley helped her put things away, but only because the teenager wanted to turn it into girl talk.

"Did you tell him everything?" Kaley asked.

"Yes, I did."

"Even that you were trying not to fall in love with him again?"

"Yes, I included that."

"What did he say?"

"At first he made a joke, but then he told me that he understood why I was being cautious."

"It's kind of sad, if you think about it."

"What do you mean?"

"Stopping yourself from loving someone."

"Please, don't steer me in the other direction." She'd convinced herself that not loving him was the right thing to do, and she didn't need Kaley pushing the issue. "I couldn't bear to fall back into that deep, dark place. Especially since I felt better after I told him."

"It still seems sad."

Victoria didn't reply. She finished hanging up her clothes and walked into the bathroom to arrange her toiletries, knowing Kaley would follow. Sure enough, the girl was right on her heels.

"How deep and dark was that place?" Kaley persisted.

"Oh, my sweet child." She sighed and touched her daughter's pretty face. "I spent years getting over Ryan. Not just because he didn't show up at the hospital, but because I missed him so badly, my bones ached."

"That's how much my dad loved my mom. And how much she loved him, too."

"Ryan and I aren't like your other parents. You can't compare us to them." Because she and Ryan would always lose.

"I know. But after you left my room last night, I started hoping that when you told him the truth, he would say that he loved you, too."

"Well, he didn't. And it's okay that he didn't." She put her toothbrush next to his, doing her best to not long for the impossible, to not break down and dream for more. "It's better if we just go our separate ways. I don't think Ryan is capable of the type of commitment I would need. I'm not even sure if I'm capable of handling it. I've kept myself apart for so long I've gotten used to being alone."

"Why does life have to be so complicated?"

"I don't know. Sometimes it just is. But let's try to enjoy the rest of our time here, okay?"

"Okay." The teenager perched on the edge of the tub. "You know what might help? If Dad could come here to meet Ryan and hang out for a few days. Then when you and I leave, Dad could fly home with us."

Clearly Kaley was trying to make sense of her disjointed family by bringing everyone together. "Sure, honey. If your dad has the time to do that, I think it would be good for all of us."

"Do you want to talk to Ryan about it or should I?"

"That's up to you."

"Then I'll do it," Kaley said. "You guys have had enough talks already."

* * *

Ryan locked up the clinic and came into the house through the back door. The kitchen was quiet, but the living room was alive with noise and energy.

Victoria was watching TV and working on her laptop, while Kaley was playing tug-of-war with Pesky. The bulldog snarled up a storm. Tug-of-war was his obsession. He set his back legs and hiked his butt in the air to get more leverage, refusing to let go. Perky was there, too, barking for added entertainment.

Ryan stood back to watch the scene, enjoying that no one had noticed him yet. This was like coming home to a family: the mom, the kid, the dogs.

He tugged a hand through his hair. A family that wasn't going to last, that didn't actually exist. The end of the week was closing in, and then Kaley and Victoria would be gone.

But they were here now, he reminded himself. Here to interact, to be part of his life.

He glanced at Victoria. He was still confused about his feelings for her. The ache from last night hadn't gone away. If anything, his turmoil grew stronger. But he was determined to never hurt her again, and that obviously meant letting her go.

He removed his lab coat, tossed it onto a side table and walked farther into the room. Perky noticed him first. She wagged her tail and ran to greet him. He petted her, rewarding her with an affectionate, "Hey, girl."

Pesky rolled his big round eyes toward Ryan, but stayed where he was, still tugging on his favorite toy, until Kaley dropped it and patted him on the head so she could jump up to see Ryan.

"How was your day?" she said.

"Good." He chuffed her chin, adoring the hell out of her. "How was yours?"

"Super. I helped Victoria move into your room, then I read a really good book, then I played on Facebook, then I started goofing around with the dogs."

"Sounds like a nice vacation day."

"It was."

He shifted his attention to Victoria. She was well aware of him now, too. Their gazes met and held.

"How was your day?" he asked.

"Mostly I worked."

"But you're settled into my room now?"

"Yes. Everything of mine is in there."

He envisioned her clothes in his closet. Had she hung the gold dress next to his suit, close enough for the garments to touch?

Kaley said, "I have something to ask you, Ryan."

He cleared his thoughts. "Sure. What is it?"

"I want my dad to come here and meet you. I was thinking that maybe he could fly in tomorrow and stay until Victoria and I leave."

Ryan's stomach dropped like an elevator. He knew that he should be gracious about meeting Eric. He owed the other man his undying gratitude for doing such a brilliant job of raising Kaley. Only why did that have to happen now? He didn't want Eric intruding on the precious time he had left with Kaley and Victoria. But he couldn't refuse his daughter's request.

"Did you talk to your dad about it yet?" he asked.

"No. I was waiting to call him until after I talked to you. He might not even be able to come on such short notice. But I thought it would be cool if he could. It

would be a great way for you to get to know him and
for all of us to spend time together."

He tried to sound enthusiastic. "Then go ahead and
call him and see what he says."

"Thanks. I will. I figured he could stay in Victoria's
old room since she's staying in your room now."

He nodded. "That will work just fine." And it was,
he supposed, his only consolation. If Eric came here
then he would see firsthand that Ryan and Victoria were
lovers.

Kaley left the room to call her dad, and the dogs
followed her. Ryan sat beside Victoria, and she turned
down the volume on the TV.

"What triggered Kaley to want her dad to visit on
this trip?" he asked.

"She's starting to get troubled about our affair. She
wants us to be like her other parents. But I told her not to
compare us to them. Things with us are too mixed-up."

"So her solution is Eric?"

"Having everyone in the same house will probably
make us seem more like a family to her."

Kaley wasn't the only one who was troubled. Ryan
was, too. His ache was getting bigger by the minute.
"Do you think having Eric here will help?"

"Yes, I do."

It wasn't helping him. But for Kaley's sake, he had
no recourse but to accept the other man and embrace
his presence. For his own sake, he secretly hoped that
Eric couldn't make it.

Kaley's sake won.

She returned, and with an elated smile she an-
nounced that her dad was flying in tomorrow.

Chapter Thirteen

What a day, Ryan thought.

Kaley had been bouncing around all afternoon, preparing for Eric's visit. She wanted to help Victoria prepare dinner tonight. Plus she and Victoria had already baked oatmeal-raisin cookies, which she said were her dad's favorite. She remarked that her mom used to make them for him and that he liked them soft and chewy.

As the hour neared for Eric to arrive, Ryan grew increasingly uncomfortable. Kaley was waiting outside on the porch, with both dogs by her side.

Ryan felt like such a jerk, begrudging Eric this visit. But he couldn't seem to help it. His masculine rivalry was on full alert. No one had asked him what his favorite cookies were. They hadn't consulted him about the dinner menu, either. They'd decided on pot roast because Eric favored meat-and-potatoes meals. Ryan appreciated that style of cooking, too, but that was beside the point.

Seriously? He was keeping score? He needed to get a grip on his emotions and stop thinking like an idiot.

He should be happy that Kaley wanted him to meet her father. Happy that Victoria was smiling at Ryan while she arranged the "Eric" cookies on a platter.

He playfully pulled her into his arms. Then he planted a loud, smacking kiss on her luscious pink lips. He liked that they were no longer hiding their affair.

She laughed, grabbed a cookie and fed it to him. The oatmeal-raisin tasted pretty darned good. They might just end up being his favorite cookies, too.

"Now I need some milk," he said.

"I'll get it for you." She removed a glass from the cabinet and opened the fridge. "I happen to know the little cow who provides it."

"Mabel is probably packing her bags as we speak, planning to sneak onto the plane and fly back to L.A. with you."

"Can't you just see her sitting there in first class with a cocktail?"

"Wearing high heels and batting her lashes? Totally."

She handed him his milk, and they laughed. He was going to be so lonely after Victoria and Kaley were gone, but he tried not to dwell on that. He forced himself to stay in a chipper mood.

They went into the living room together. The house was clean as a whistle. In addition to helping with the cookies, their daughter had dusted and swept and ran the vacuum.

He said, "Kaley is certainly excited about seeing her dad."

"They were already a close-knit family, and then she and Eric became even closer after Corrine died. He's her rock."

"That's understandable." To keep his envy in check, he added, "I'm looking forward to meeting him."

"I'm so glad that you feel that way. I often think about how it would have been if the adoption had been open. We would have known Eric and Corrine from the start. They would have been part of our lives, along with Kaley." She glanced out the window.

So did Ryan, getting a glimpse of their daughter waiting on the porch. Sitting there like that, she looked younger than her eighteen years. Her hair was plaited into a single braid with ribbons woven through it, and she was leaning her elbows against her knees. He envisioned her as a child, skinning those knees and elbows, then sniffing back tears as her mommy and daddy bandaged them.

Victoria continued talking. "I also spent a lot of years thinking about how it would have been if I'd been able to keep her. Would I have been able to provide for her? Would I have struggled to be a good mom, with I-told-you-sos from my parents? Or would I have proved them wrong?"

"I think you would have proved them wrong. You even proved them wrong by searching for Kaley and becoming a strong influence in her life now."

"She's influenced by you, too."

But he would never be like Eric. No matter how many years passed or how close he and Kaley became, he could never compete with her father. Even Victoria had told Kaley not to compare her and Ryan to Eric and Corrine.

"How much time did you spend imagining us married and raising her by ourselves?" he asked, pushing the conversation in a deeper direction.

"Too much time. But that was when I was pregnant. I stopped picturing us together after she was born."

"You were smart to let those fantasies go. You deserved better."

She blinked, turned, looked at him. "You don't have to keep beating yourself up about the past, Ryan. You've done what you could to help me heal."

A healing that wasn't working, he thought. Not for either of them. Victoria no longer wanted to spend the rest of her life with him, and he was afraid of analyzing his feelings for her.

Why? Because he didn't trust himself not to screw up again? Because he'd never been good at love?

The front door flew open and Kaley poked her head inside. "He's here!"

Ryan jumped to his feet. He could see Eric's shuttle pulling up out front.

"We'll be right there, honey," Victoria said.

"That's okay. I'll bring him inside." Kaley dashed down the porch steps.

Ryan and Victoria stood at the front door. Eric exited the van. Ryan recognized him from his photos. With his casual urban attire and short tousled haircut, he had the look of an art teacher, which was exactly what he was.

He appeared to be in his young-forties and was about Ryan's height and with a similar build. His mixed-blood heritage was obvious with his bronzed skin, dark brown hair and strong-edged features. Ryan's was just as apparent, but Eric wore his with the confidence of a man who knew his culture. Ryan was still learning what being Native meant.

Kaley ran into Eric's arms, and he hugged her. No one would ever know that she wasn't his biological child. They looked natural together.

Eric had brought one small overnight bag that was looped around his shoulder. But he was only staying for a few days. Then all of them would be gone, and Ryan would be alone.

"Kaley really needs for him to be here," Victoria said, as father and daughter separated from their hug.

"Yes, I can see how much this means to her." It was apparent that she needed the emotional stability that only Eric could provide.

A few minutes later, the four of them gathered in the entryway, and the women stood back while the men shook hands and introduced themselves.

Ryan paid the other dad a compliment, giving credit where credit was due. "You certainly raised Kaley right. She's as perfect as a daughter can be."

"Thank you. She's my pride and joy. And I'm happy that she has gotten to know you and Victoria. Her mom would be thrilled about this. It's turning into the open adoption she always wanted."

Except that Corrine was gone and Kaley was an adult now. But everyone knew how much time had passed. That went without saying.

Eric smiled at Victoria. "Hey, *Gigage*."

"Hey." She reached forward.

As they embraced, Ryan puzzled over the unusual name Eric had called her. He considered their hug, too, and how comfortable they seemed with each other. But he'd expected as much.

"Come on, Dad." Kaley beamed. "I'll show you to your room. Then I'll take you outside so you can meet Mabel and Thor."

"Oh, that's right." Eric chuckled. "The miniature cow and the draft horse. You told me about them over the phone." He turned to Ryan. "This is a great place, by the way. Who wouldn't love having an old farmhouse?"

"Thanks. I like it." But the impending emptiness was gnawing at him, chewing clean through to his mixed-up heart.

Kaley took Eric upstairs, and Ryan said to Victoria, "What does *gigage* mean?"

"It's 'red' in Cherokee."

"He nicknamed you that because of your hair?"

She nodded.

Red was a common reference to redheads, but the Cherokee spin personalized it. "When did he start calling you that?"

"Soon after we became friends. He always wondered if one of Kaley's parents was a redhead because of the auburn in her hair. It's really strong in the sun."

"Yes, I know. I noticed it on the day I met her, when we were standing outside by the car. It's beautiful." He noticed that Victoria's was sleek and straight today. "And so is yours, no matter how you style it."

"You always make me feel good about my hair. You make me feel good about a lot of things."

But sometimes he made her feel bad, too. Trying to banish the badness, he kissed her, hard and deep, thriving on the much-needed flavor of her mouth.

She seemed to thrive on his, too. She moaned beneath his aggressive onslaught.

When it ended, she said, "You taste like dessert."

From the "Eric" cookie he'd eaten. He frowned, imagining her kissing the other man with the same savoring indulgence.

Kaley and her dad returned. But only long enough to head for the back door and out to see Ryan's animals.

Everything at the farm belonged to Ryan. Everything and nothing, he thought. After Victoria and Kaley went home, he would be rattling around by himself, with memories of the last two weeks bumping in and out of his mind.

No, not just the past two weeks. The past twenty years. That was how long ago he'd first met Victoria.

Suddenly he wanted to pull her into his arms and beg her to stay. But what right did he have to ask her to give up her life for him? He was still too afraid to figure out if he loved her, let alone be the kind of man she deserved. What if he broke her heart again? What if he destroyed what was left of it?

"You seem distracted," she said.

He was. Very. "Do you remember the day we first met?"

"When I was bending over the water fountain at school and you were checking out my butt?"

He managed a smile. "Yeah. What a view." But the memory that struck him the most was when she'd turned around and caught him looking at her. "Remember how we stared at each other?"

"I was so embarrassed. I think I had water dribbling out of my mouth."

"Are you kidding? You were the prettiest thing I'd ever seen. The shiest, too."

"That day changed me forever. I think I fell in love with you right then and there."

He wished that she still loved him. "Being with you changed me, too." The girl with whom he'd lost his virginity. The girl who'd had his baby.

Before he could steal another kiss, Kaley and her dad came back from the barn, and she directed Eric to the cookies.

He ate four of them, praising her new baking skills and saying how scrumptious they were.

"You'll have to make these again when we get home," he said.

"Only if Victoria helps me again."

"Of course I will," came the mom reply.

Ryan listened to the three of them make plans that didn't include him, and it hurt like hell.

Later, while dinner was being prepared, Ryan and Eric sat on the patio. Ryan glanced at the laurel tree and the feminine sway of its branches. Who knew a tree could be so womanlike?

Eric said, "My baby has been having a wonderful time here."

His baby. For a minute, it almost sounded as if he were talking about Victoria. But that was only because Ryan had been imagining her as part of the tree.

He switched his thoughts to Kaley and replied, "I'm going to miss her when she leaves. It won't be the same around here without her."

"I know what you mean. I'm going to miss her when she's off at school. She wants to live in a dorm instead of staying home. She wants the full college experience. But I want her to make the most of it, too." He smiled. "No doubt she'll come home on the weekends to do her laundry, though."

Ryan wished that she would be coming home to his

house instead. That she'd chosen a university in Oregon. But she'd already decided on a school long before she'd met him. "I invited her spend time with me on her breaks."

"She told me. That would be great."

Yes, but would it happen? Her first college break would be winter and that would entail Christmas. He suspected that she would want to spend the holiday with Eric and Victoria.

Eric and Victoria.

Already they sounded like a couple. But they weren't, he reminded himself. For now, she was still sharing Ryan's bed.

When Victoria came outside to tell them dinner was ready, he got the same thunderstruck feeling he'd gotten at the water fountain that day.

But once they went inside and dived into the food, he felt her slipping away from him. She laughed and talked easily with Eric and Kaley.

Ryan forced himself to join in, trying to seem as if he was enjoying himself, too. He didn't want to spoil the moment for everyone else.

Even if he was lost in confusion.

As Ryan brushed his teeth and got ready for bed that night, he decided that he was going to continue to do everything in his power to hide his feelings and make the last few days of Victoria and Kaley's trip a positive experience.

He left the bathroom and crossed the threshold into his bedroom. Victoria was already in bed, and with her fair skin and bright hair, she looked like a siren.

A wood nymph. He would always think of her that way.

As if under her spell, he moved forward, got into bed and lay beside her.

As impossible as it was, he wished that he'd married her when he'd had the chance. No, he thought. That wasn't a good wish. He would have been a terrible husband. He hadn't even been a good husband to Jackie, and he'd been older and more mature when he'd married her.

"It turned out to be a really nice day," Victoria said. "Just what Kaley needed. Her family having fun together."

Ryan tried not to feel guilty for the facade, for the fun he hadn't had. "Do you think we seem less mixed-up to her now?"

Victoria nodded. "It's better now that Eric is here. He has a way of keeping her grounded."

"The love between them is palpable."

"Can you imagine how wonderful that must feel? We didn't get that from our parents."

"That's part of what makes us so mixed-up, Tore."

"I agree. We're products of our environments." She furrowed her brow. "I always wanted to be loved like that."

He touched the top of her hand. She'd given so much to the people she'd loved and barely received anything in return. "I should have loved you. I should have given you what you needed."

Her voice hitched. "I wasn't referring to you. I was talking about my parents."

"I know. But I still should have."

"It's better that we've gotten past that."

Ryan wasn't past it. Everything inside him hurt. It was strange, too, because he couldn't remember ever feeling this tortured over Jackie, not even when she'd said that she wanted to divorce him.

He said, "I'll bet your parents would be upset if they knew you were in my bed. Do they even know you and Kaley are visiting me?"

"Yes, and they thought it was a terrible idea. But they never support anything I do. I wonder what your dad would have thought."

"Of you and Kaley visiting me? Or of you being back in my bed?"

"Both."

Ryan considered his old man. "He was still grumpy right up to the end, but I think he would have liked Kaley. I think she would have charmed him." He shifted to look at her. "He liked you, too, Tore. He just didn't like that we got pregnant."

She frowned straight at him. "*We* didn't get pregnant, Ryan. *I* got pregnant."

He winced. "Sorry. I've just heard other people say that." Committed couples, he realized. Not people who'd been through what they'd been through.

"I'm sorry, too. I didn't mean to reprimand you. It just struck a chord, I guess." She gentled her voice. "But I don't want to keep dwelling on the past or saying hurtful things to each other."

"Me, neither." He'd promised himself that he was going to hide his feelings and not drag her into his mess. "Let's focus on something else."

"How about sleep?" She curled up against him, her body soft and warm. "I'm getting tired, and it's always so peaceful in your arms."

He wondered how she could find peace in the arms of a man she refused to love. But he didn't question it. He simply held her, keeping her close.

The following day Ryan had a full schedule at the clinic. He finally locked up around six. As far as he knew, Victoria and Kaley had taken Eric on a tour of the town, but they should be back by now.

Only as he crossed the property, he saw Eric and Victoria coming from the edge of the woods, without Kaley being anywhere in sight.

Ryan's heart went ballistic. The woods were *his* place with Victoria. She was *his* nymph. What right did Eric have to intrude on that?

Suddenly everything he'd been feeling, all of the pain and confusion, crashed like a tidal wave. He turned on his heel and headed toward them.

He tried to tell himself to calm down, to stop, to take a breath. But his ego wouldn't listen. The devastation was too deep. At that soul-crushing moment, he couldn't bear to let Victoria go, not without a fight.

Because he loved her.

It was a hell of a time to figure it out, a horrible time to feel it. Consumed with the realization of being in love and seeing her with Eric, he kept storming in their direction.

For now, Victoria still belonged to Ryan. She'd slept in his arms last night. She'd cuddled with him. Eric was moving in on Ryan's territory before Ryan's bed was even empty.

He caught up with them and made a beeline for Kaley's dad. "You've got a lot of nerve."

Eric flinched. "What?"

"Going off into the woods with my woman."

Victoria reacted, jumping in before Eric could respond. "Oh, my God, Ryan. How can you say something like that? How can you even think it?"

"What else am I supposed to think? Seeing you alone with him?"

"We weren't alone. Kaley was with us, but she went back to the house. But even if we had gone off alone, there would have been nothing wrong with that." The god-awful expression in her eyes said it all. She was mortified that he thought so little of her.

Instantly ashamed of his outburst, Ryan took the breath he should have taken before he'd flown off the handle. But that didn't keep his pulse from spinning or his voice from quavering. He was still an emotional mess. "I'm sorry. I've just been so afraid that you two were going to get together someday." He included Eric in the apology, meeting the other man's gaze. "I've been feeling things I didn't expect to feel, and it's been so confusing."

Victoria remained spitting mad. No forgiveness. No empathy. "Everything is always about you, Ryan."

"It's all right." Eric came to Ryan's defense. "He said he was sorry."

"I don't care how sorry he is." She was shouting now. "He had no right to accuse us of behaving badly." She took a step toward Ryan. "You're the same person you always were."

He wanted to die. To sink to the ground. The same boy who'd hurt her. The same man who was hurting her now. "I swear this is the last thing I ever meant to do."

"Then you shouldn't have done it."

"No, I shouldn't have." But as long as he was standing here, with nothing left but his heart oozing all over his sleeve, he said, "I know you're going to probably want to kick me in the teeth for saying this, but I love you, Tore."

She gaped at him. "Since when?"

He swallowed the lump in his throat. "It just—"

"It just what, Ryan? Occurred to you when you saw me and Eric together? When you decided that he might steal me away?" She looked capable of slapping him, even if she didn't do it. "I don't want your phony, jealous love."

"It isn't phony." It was as real as anything he'd ever known. "And I'm sorry about the jealousy."

"I don't believe that you love me, and I don't need this kind of torment." She pushed past him and walked away, going toward the house.

Ryan didn't follow her. He knew enough to let her go off by herself. But he wished that she would have slapped him. He wished she would have left a stinging handprint on his cheek.

Eric was still standing there, an unexpected ally. "Just for the record, there's nothing between Victoria and me. Nor will there ever be."

"I know." Ryan had manifested it in his mind, letting it fester until the poison had bubbled over. "It was my insecurity."

"Also for the record, I believe that you love her."

He nearly staggered. "You do?"

"Yes, but I'm not going to try to convince her to be with you. I don't think she would listen to me, anyway."

"I don't think so, either." Because no else could fix

what Ryan had broken. But the worst part was that Ryan didn't know if he could fix it, or if the pain he kept causing Victoria was beyond repair.

Chapter Fourteen

Victoria rushed upstairs and burst into tears. And just as she was about dash into her room to hide from the world, Kaley came out of her room, trapping Victoria in the hallway.

"What's wrong?"

"It's nothing I can't handle." A lie if she ever told one. She wasn't anywhere near handling it.

"I've never seen you cry like that. I've never seen you cry at all. Please, tell me what happened."

"It was just something with Ryan."

"What? Tell me. I want to know."

She wasn't quite sure how to relay it to her eighteen-year-old daughter without it sounding more humiliating than it already was. "He thought there was something going on between me and your dad."

Kaley's jaw dropped. "Why would he think that?"

"He's been jealous all along, worried that my friendship with your dad was going to turn romantic. Once he realized he was wrong, he apologized, but it still makes me feel awful."

"Is my dad mad at Ryan?"

"No. He accepted his apology."

"Do you want me to be mad at Ryan? Because if you do, I will be. I'll take your side."

"Oh, honey." Victoria wiped her tears. Kaley was approaching it as a war between the sexes. But it went so much deeper than that. "I don't want you to be mad at anyone. This isn't about taking sides."

Kaley didn't reply.

Victoria's tears rushed back. "He told me that he loved me."

"Oh, my God. What's wrong with that?"

"I don't think it's genuine. I think he got so caught up in his jealousy, he only thinks he loves me."

"And you're afraid that when his supposed love wears off, you'll be hurt all over again?"

"Yes."

"I would probably feel that way, too, if it was me. Ryan has done a lot of things that hurt you. Are you sure you don't want me to be mad at him?"

"I'm sure."

Kaley seemed perplexed. "If I can't be mad, then what am I supposed to do?"

"You're not supposed to do anything."

"Maybe I'm supposed to talk you into forgiving him."

Definitely not that. "No, honey, you're not."

The determined teen played devil's advocate, anyway. "What if you're too upset to see the truth? What if he really does love you? How will you ever know if you don't give him a chance?"

Victoria had a ready answer, painful as it was. But everything connected with Ryan caused her pain. "I'm not strong enough to get over him a second time if it doesn't work. I just can't do it."

"I think you can."

"I appreciate your confidence, but I need to get away from here. I'm going to check into a motel until it's time to leave." To be alone with her tears, with her fears, with a past that refused to die.

"What should Dad and I do?"

"You can stay here with Ryan. You can keep him company." The last thing she wanted was to punish Ryan or take his daughter away. As angry as he was at him, she was angry at herself, too. She'd known better than to fall back into his bed. But she'd caved in to temptation, and now she was paying the price.

Kaley asked, "Will you call me when you get to the motel and let me know you're okay?"

"I course I will." She drew Kaley into her arms, holding the child she'd conceived with Ryan.

Before she packed her bags and left him behind.

Victoria had gone without saying goodbye, leaving a big gaping hole in Ryan's heart. And now he was occupying the front porch with Eric and Kaley while dusk blanketed the sky.

"I just thought of something I hadn't thought of before." Kaley sat cross-legged on the wood planks, facing Ryan and her dad. "Did I influence you?"

"What do you mean?" Ryan gave her a baffled look.

"Did you get jealous of my dad because of what I

kept saying about me wanting him to date? Did you think that I wanted him to date Victoria?"

Ryan gently replied, "Everything that happened is my fault, and mine alone. You aren't responsible for any of it."

Eric said, "Hold on. Wait a minute." He addressed Kaley. "What's this bit about you wanting me to date?"

She sighed. "You need to have a life, Dad. You need to find someone and be happy again."

"Please, don't tell me what I need to do."

"Dang, you're stubborn. Both of you are stubborn and stupid." She ganged up on her dads. "Male and macho, screwing up your lives."

Clearly, Eric begged to differ. "I haven't screwed anything up."

She argued. "Being alone the way you are isn't healthy. And you." She made a chin gesture toward Ryan. "Sitting here instead of chasing after Victoria. I already told you where she is staying. I even got her room number for you. How much more incentive do you need?"

"I plan on going to the motel to see her. I'm just giving her time to calm down." To be sure he said the right thing, did the right thing.

"You're just scared."

Hell, yes, he was scared. He was petrified. His stomach was tied up in knots. He had no idea if she would ever speak to him again, let alone believe that he loved her.

"Kaley," Eric said. "I appreciate that you're worried about me and that you're concerned about Ryan and Victoria, but you aren't qualified to dole out this type of advice."

"Victoria told me that sex is better when you love someone."

Her father nearly tipped over in his chair. "I do not want to discuss sex with you. Not here. Not now." He then added, "But Victoria is right, it's better for women when they're in love."

"But it isn't better for men? Jeez, Dad, nothing like teaching me about double standards."

"I wasn't… I'm not…" He looked to Ryan for help.

Ryan shook his head. He wasn't going to get in any deeper than he already was. Eric was on his own with this particular discussion.

"Have you been with anyone since Mom died?" she asked him.

Eric blanched. "That's none of your business."

"Just tell me."

"Leave it alone, Kaley."

She pounded her fists onto the porch. "Like I said, stubborn." She stood up. "I'm going for a walk before all of this this male stupidity rubs off on me."

She called the dogs and they went with her, trotting off as if they agreed that all XY-chromosome humans were imbeciles.

After she was out of sight, Ryan glanced at the other man, and they burst into nervous laughter, feeling as dumb as they probably were.

As soon as they sobered, Eric said, "There's something I should probably tell you that I haven't told Kaley or Victoria. It's actually about you and Victoria."

Ryan tried to prepare himself for whatever it was. He just hoped it wasn't something bad. "Go on."

"I didn't want Kaley to search for her birth parents."

Damn. That was bad. "I thought you and Corrine encouraged her to look for us. I thought you planted that seed a long time ago."

"We did. But this goes back to the open adoption. I had some reservations at first. I was uncertain about having the birth mother or birth parents involved. What if he or she interfered with our family values? What it they made things difficult? Or what if they were amazing people and our child wanted to spend more time with them than with us? That actually worried me the most. I didn't want to compete for my child's affection."

Ah. The reason was unfolding.

Eric continued. "Corrine helped me get past my reservations. She'd struggled with her identity, and she didn't want our child to experience that same sense of loss. She convinced me that having the birth parents involved would better our child's life and would create balance in ours. We even met with other families who had these types of arrangements. And the more I learned about it, the more I knew that an open adoption was the right choice for us."

Ryan interjected. "But then fate intervened and the first newborn that became available to you was being offered through a closed adoption."

"Yes. Our little Kaley. Once she was old enough to understand, we discussed the adoption and told her that she could search for her birth parents if she ever felt the need." He paused, frowned. "Only I never imagined that my wife would be gone when it happened or that I would be having those old reservations again. It didn't seem fair that I had to welcome strangers in my life, not after everything I'd been through."

"I don't blame you for feeling that way."

"I came to terms with it, which is why I forgave you

so easily when you were jealous of me. I've had to work on not being envious of you or Victoria, on graciously sharing my daughter with you."

Touched by Eric's candor, Ryan said, "I'm glad it was you who became Kaley's father, and I'll never begrudge you a moment of your time with her, not ever again." He only hoped that he could be half the dad Eric was. "I'll never begrudge your friendship with Victoria, either. And as long as we're spilling our guts, I have to admit that there were times that I thought you were better suited to Victoria than I was. You just seemed so perfect."

"I let my daughter believe that I was happy about her searching for her birth parents when I wasn't. There's nothing perfect about that."

"Are you going to tell Kaley the truth now?"

"I'll talk to her later tonight." Eric glanced in the direction of where Kaley and the dogs were walking. "Hopefully she will be in a better mood by then." He looked up at the sky. "I wonder if it's going to rain. Clouds are starting to gather."

"It's hard to say. It comes and goes so quickly."

"Did it rain the day Kaley was born?"

"No, it didn't." But it should have. Tears from heaven, Ryan thought. Tears he'd been too afraid to cry. "That was the worst day of my life."

"And the best day of mine. It's bittersweet, isn't it?"

Ryan nodded. Then suddenly the clarity that had been missing came barreling into his mind.

Boom. Bang. Like a bullet to the heart. The day Kaley was born. The reason he'd panicked instead of going to the hospital.

The reason for everything.

* * *

A knock sounded on Victoria's motel room door, and she leaped up to check the peephole.

Ryan was on the other side.

Should she answer it or ignore him? He knocked again. No doubt he could see her shadow beneath the door.

Her leery shadow. She went ahead and opened the door a crack, feeling far too vulnerable. Her eyes were puffy from the tears she'd shed. She willed herself not to cry while he was standing there.

"You shouldn't be here," she said.

"I couldn't stay away." He sounded as if he would've followed her to the ends of the earth. "I meant what I said about loving you."

"And I meant what I said about not believing you."

"Let me prove it. Give me a chance."

She hesitated, cautious of letting down her guard. "By talking your way back into my good graces? Words are cheap."

"Not the right words. Not the truth. Please, just one chance."

Victoria could barely breathe. She was afraid of giving him a chance, of getting sucked into the painful vortex that was Ryan. But if she sent him away, how would she ever know if his love might actually be real? Even Kaley had mentioned that.

She gestured for him to come inside, but she didn't allow him to feel welcome. She didn't offer him a place to sit, nor did she sit herself.

While they stood in the middle of the cramped room, he hooked his thumbs in his jeans pockets, a gesture leftover from their youth, reminding her of the untamed teenager he'd been.

He said, "I figured out why I panicked that day."

Victoria's pulse punched its way to her heart. "You panicked because you couldn't handle the situation."

"Yes, but I couldn't handle it because I loved you, even back then. And somewhere in my subconscious, I was afraid of giving up our child because I knew it meant that I was giving you up, too. I think deep down I wanted a future with you and our baby as much you wanted it. Only I was too young and scared to know that's what I wanted or how to make it work."

She clutched her middle. She'd been young and scared, too.

He added, "It's also why my marriage failed. Jackie was right when she said that I didn't love her enough to give her the family she craved. How could I when I'd lost the family I'd craved, when you and Kaley were out there, floating in a sea of painful memories?"

Such prose, she thought. Such poetic angst. He was good with his words. He'd learned how to say all the right things.

The truth, as he called it.

Was it the truth? Had sixteen-year-old Ryan been in love with her? Had he secretly longed to be a father as much as she longed to be a mother?

He said, "My dad kept saying how important it was for us to give up the baby and never see it again. He convinced me that we were too immature to become parents. That it would better if our child never knew us. So I compensated by suppressing the love I had for you and detaching myself from the baby. But on the day she was born, I lost it and had a breakdown."

Victoria wanted to believe his story. She wanted so desperately to accept it. But she was still wary.

"You're making me weak," she said.

"I'm trying to create strength between us, Tore."

Was it possible to be strong? In her estimation love made people weak. She'd lost her power when she'd fallen in love with him.

He spoke again. "I want to give you everything. Everything a husband can give his wife. But I want you to feel safe with me. That's the most important thing."

Victoria teetered on her feet. "Is this a proposal?"

"Yes. It's my vow to love and honor you for the rest of our lives."

He made it so sound simple, but she knew it wasn't. "I don't know what to say. I don't even know what to feel." Not when her knees were about to buckle.

He reached out to touch her cheek. "Then think about it and come to me with an answer. And whatever it is, I'll accept it. I can't force you to be with me. I can't insist that you love me again. I can only hope and pray that you will."

The weakness got stronger. Or was it her who was getting stronger? She didn't know. But by God, his touch felt good.

So beautifully good. But instead of falling into his arms, she took a step back. "You better go now."

"However long it takes, I'll be waiting." He walked to the door, then turned and looked at her. "I honest-to-God love you. I swear I do."

She watched him go, tempted to call him back, to commit to him on the spot, to agree to become his loving, caring wife. But she didn't do it. Victoria wasn't going to rush into the most important decision of her life.

Chapter Fifteen

Ryan waited throughout the rest of the day and into the evening. He waited through a restless night of sleep and into the morning.

He went outside to do his chores and returned to the breakfast table to find Eric and Kaley there, eating cereal. They'd set a bowl out for him, too. His daughter and her father were fast becoming his closest family. Now all Ryan needed was Victoria back in the fold, back in his life.

He needed her with every breath in his body. But did she need him, too? So far, the odds weren't in his favor.

"I made coffee," Eric said.

"Thank you." Ryan poured himself a cup and fixed it the way he liked it. He noticed that Kaley was drinking the gourmet stuff.

"Have you heard from her?" the anxious teenager asked.

"No. Not a word."

"Me, neither. Not since you went over there." She ate a mouthful of the crunchy fiber in her bowl.

Ryan doused his with milk. The waiting was killing him. But he'd told Victoria that he would wait for as long as it took, and he meant it. But, still. Was this how she'd felt, waiting for him at the hospital? He couldn't fathom how she'd gotten through it. "I feel like I'm on death row and waiting for a stay of execution."

Kaley wagged her spoon at him. "You need to think positive." She went after another bite. "Let's think positive together. Let's transmit good energy. Let's say things that will make Victoria want to marry you."

"Okay," he told her. "You go first." He needed all the help he could get.

She closed her eyes, as if she were making a wish. Then she opened them and said, "When you get married, I'll be the maid of honor at your wedding. I'll wear a Paiute-inspired dress with fringe and beads and pretty embellishments."

"That's sounds really nice." Ryan appreciated the image she'd implanted in his mind. "But the wedding details will be up to Victoria." The wedding he prayed would happen.

"I think she'll like my idea." Kaley's confidence was obviously part of her positive efforts, part of trying to make it happen. "But it doesn't matter what the details are, as long as she becomes your wife. I'd wear a gunnysack if that's what she wanted me to wear."

"So would I," Ryan said, and laughed at the visual it presented.

Eric chuckled, too. "I wore a tux at my wedding. And I looked damn fine."

"Show-off," Ryan replied, keeping the silly banter going. It was better than sitting there in clock-ticking silence.

Kaley studied Ryan from beneath her fancy coffee. "Dad told me what he told you yesterday."

About Eric not wanting her to search for him and Victoria. "It's been a tough road for all of us. Learning to connect the way we have."

"And look how great it turned out for me." More positive affirmations. "I mean, really, how lucky can a girl get, having two weird dads?"

Both men laughed. But they exchanged a meaningful glance, too. They were indeed a family. But without Victoria, a piece of Ryan would always be missing.

"Do you really think it will be okay?" he asked Kaley.

"Yes," she responded with conviction. "I do."

Victoria went crazy, thinking and rethinking her decision, going over every single thing Ryan had said. She went over every aspect of her life, too, and the years she'd spent missing him, needing him, loving him. Nothing could bring those years back, except for being with him now.

She arrived at his house during his evening chores, certain she would find him alone in the barn.

She was right. He was milking Mabel. But he didn't know she was there. She'd entered quietly, taking a moment to study him. He looked like the country boy he was, with his dark denim clothes and rugged work boots.

Finally when he finished filling the bucket, he stood up and turned around.

"Victoria." Her name spilled from his lips. He nearly spilled the milk, too. He set the bucket on the ground.

She could tell that his breath was lodged in his throat. But she was having the same reaction. Hers was stuck, too.

"I have something for you." She handed him the package she was carrying.

He opened it, discovering the wedding basket. He looked expectantly at her. "What does this mean? That you want to marry me? Or that you're returning it because you don't want to marry me and you can't bear to keep it?"

He already knew that she'd hated the basket when she'd first gotten it. Was he wondering if she still hated it?

She put his mind at ease. "It means that I love you and I want to be your bride. And I believe that you love me, too." He wasn't her weakness. He was her heart, her future, the father of her child. "I understand how you felt when we were young. I understand your fear and your panic. And I understand how it affected your marriage to Jackie, too. We've both let the past dictate our unhappiness." But now they had a second chance of being truly joyful.

He moved closer, still clutching the basket, holding it tight against his body. "Where do you want to live? Where do you want to start over? Should I move to California or do you want to move here?"

She'd never considered him relocating to California. Nor was she considering it now. "I want to stay here." She made a wide gesture. "At the farm." She didn't want to take him away from his house or his animals or the practice he'd built. She wanted to be part of it. "It will be like coming full circle. Us in our hometown, together where we belong."

He smiled. "Kaley wants to wear a Paiute-inspired dress at the ceremony." He explained the positive affirmations their daughter had suggested. "She was trying so hard to convince me that it could happen."

"And now it is." She loved the idea of Kaley's dress. "I can see her coming down the aisle in feathers, fringe and flowers. Our baby, all grown up." She thought back to the day she was born. "If only I'd known then what I know now."

"Then? You mean at the hospital?"

She nodded. "If I'd had a crystal ball, I would have seen her being part of our lives. I would have seen that you loved me, too."

"You see it now."

"Yes, I do." Deep within his eyes.

He came forward to hug her, the wedding basket between them. If Kaley was going to wear a Native dress, then the basket was going to be part of the ceremony, too.

She said, "Let's get married here on the farm."

"When?"

"How about next summer? That will give us plenty of time to plan it." She envisioned herself as his bride. "Maybe I can have my dress embellished with Native accents in honor of your heritage. But some of the beads on my gown can be gold. And I can carry a bouquet of white roses, glittered in gold, like the corsage you gave me."

"Gold is your power, Victoria. Like Eros's arrow."

"The god of love." She put her head on his shoulder, breathing in his hay-and-animal scent. She'd loved him for most of her life, even when she was trying not to love him.

"What sort of ring do you want?"

"I don't know." Just knowing that she was going to have a ring made her wonderfully dizzy. She was actually going to marry Ryan Nash, the boy of her dreams. She nuzzled him, and in the background Mabel mooed. Victoria smiled against his skin.

He turned his head and captured her mouth. And oh, the taste of him, so spicy, so darkly romantic. What a sexy husband she was going to have.

Breathless, they separated. Was her lipstick smeared? She'd applied it carefully before she'd come over. She'd made herself look as pretty as she could for him.

"What about kids, Tore?"

She blinked, then realized he was asking about raising a family with her. She answered, "I hope this makes sense, but I think we should wait to have more children. I think we need more time."

"I'm glad you said that because I think so, too." He explained his reasoning. "Our relationship with Kaley is still forming. We're still new parents, even if our daughter was born eighteen years ago. Later, we can have other kids. But for now, we need only her. And each other."

She couldn't have said it better herself. Because they shared the same past, the same tortured love, the same turmoil, the same inability to heal—until now.

Victoria prolonged her departure. On the day she'd been scheduled to leave, she remained in Oregon. Soon she would go back to California and start packing to move here for good. But she wasn't ready to fly out just yet.

Eric and Kaley were leaving, though. Eric had arranged for a shuttle, and they were waiting for it to arrive.

Kaley kept hugging Victoria. The teenager was all smiles. During one of the hugs, she said, "I'm so happy for you, *mi otra madre*."

My other mother. Victoria would never tire of hearing that, and it was especially wonderful today.

Kaley continued by saying, "I wanted you and Ryan to be together. It couldn't have worked out more perfectly."

Victoria held her daughter's hand. "I'm so excited about moving here, but I'm going to miss living near you."

"You and Ryan can visit as often as you want, and I'll come back and see you as much as I can. Dad will, too." She glanced over at Eric. "Won't you, Dad?"

"Absolutely," her father replied. He was gathering Kaley's luggage and putting it by the front door. "I'll wear out my welcome."

Victoria laughed. "You could never do that. You're having a bromance with Ryan."

Her fiancé—oh, how wonderful that sounded—caught wind of the joke. He good-naturedly said, "I can't help if I have a thing for the guy who raised my kid."

"Likewise," Eric replied. "With the guy who sired mine."

"The farmer's daughter." Ryan teased Kaley and came over to pull on the gingham top she happened to be wearing.

"They're such dorks," the teen said, swatting him away.

"Lovable dorks." Victoria knew Kaley was thrilled to have two daddies who doted on her.

Ryan walked over to Eric. "All kidding aside, I have something to ask you."

"Sure, shoot."

"How would you feel about being my best man? I know it's still a ways off, but I'd be honored to have you stand up for me."

"And I'd be honored to do it." They clasped hands, then went for a slightly awkward hug.

"Definitely a bromance," Kaley said with a quick roll of her eyes, although everyone could see how pleased she was.

Victoria was pleased, too. But who wouldn't be? Happiness radiated from their daughter. Of course Kaley was still concerned about Eric being alone, but she'd promised not to bug him about it. Victoria suspected that Kaley was going to be thinking all sorts of positive thoughts about Eric finding a mate. But it was Eric who had to want it. Eric who had to allow another woman into his heart, just as she and Ryan had allowed each other into theirs.

When the airport van arrived, tender hugs and loving goodbyes were exchanged. Ryan held Kaley close, and Victoria suspected that he was imagining himself holding her as a newborn. He kissed her forehead, and she smiled at him.

Eric reached for Victoria, and they embraced. He said, "Be well, *Gigage*. Be happy."

"You, too. And thank you, Eric."

"For what?"

"For sharing Kaley with us."

"It's my pleasure. Ryan is like a brother to me now, and you're my little red-haired sister."

To prove his point, he gave one of her wild curls a sibling-style tug. She was wearing her hair natural today because she'd showered with Ryan that morning and after they'd gotten wonderfully wet, he'd towel-dried her hair for her. The entire process had been divine.

"Ryan is a good man," Eric said, clearly aware of the romance in her eyes. "He'll make a good husband."

Just as Eric had been a good husband to Corrine. "I'm glad he chose you for his best man."

"And I'm glad he chose you for his bride."

After a moment of silence, she said, "I'll see you and Kaley when I come back to pack my things. I already called my apartment and gave my thirty-day notice to move."

"Anxious, are you?" He smiled. "That's how it should be."

Was he hiding behind his smile? Was he thinking about how anxious he and Corrine had been to be together? Was he thinking about his beautiful lost wife? Victoria had never been to Corrine's grave, but Kaley had told her that Eric went there often, bringing flowers to the site. Kaley did, too, but not as frequently as her father.

Eric stepped back and turned toward Ryan. The men shook hands, and Eric said something to Ryan in Cherokee. Then he leaned in close and quietly translated it. Victoria couldn't hear what it was.

As the driver loaded the luggage, she and Kaley hugged for one last time that day, then father and daughter climbed into the shuttle.

Off they went, with Kaley waving madly from the window.

Her birth parents stood in the front yard and waved back, sending their sweet girl back to California with her adoptive daddy.

After the van disappeared down the road, Ryan said, "Eric told me that you and I walk in each other's souls. That's what he said in his language. It's what the Cherokee say when someone loves someone. That they walk in that person's soul."

Victoria's eyes turned misty. "I'm going to walk there forever, Ryan."

He met her gaze, his deep brown eyes focused lovingly on hers. "And I'll walk in yours forever, too."

He kissed her, soft and slow, and she savored the feeling, luxuriating in wonder and warmth. A light breeze blew, the earth enveloping them in its beauty.

In the distance, the trees made their powerful mark, the woods alive with birds and butterflies and plants that grew vibrant and free.

Home, Victoria thought.

Ryan kissed her again, running his hands along the sides of her body and following her curves with his fingers, claiming her with the confidence of a man who knew that the woman in his arms belonged to him.

Victoria was exactly where she wanted to be.

* * * * *

A sneaky peek at next month…

Cherish™

ROMANCE TO MELT THE HEART EVERY TIME

My wish list for next month's titles…

In stores from 20th September 2013:

☐ The Christmas Baby Surprise – Shirley Jump

& A Weaver Beginning – Allison Leigh

☐ Single Dad's Christmas Miracle – Susan Meier

& Snowbound with the Soldier – Jennifer Faye

In stores from 4th October 2013:

☐ A Maverick for Christmas – Leanne Banks

& Her Montana Christmas Groom – Teresa Southwick

☐ The Redemption of Rico D'Angelo – Michelle Douglas

& The Rancher's Christmas Princess – Christine Rimmer

Available at WHSmith, Tesco, Asda, Eason, Amazon and Apple

Just can't wait?

Visit us Online

You can buy our books online a month before they hit the shops! **www.millsandboon.co.uk**

0913/23

Wrap up warm this winter with Sarah Morgan...

Sleigh Bells in the Snow

Kayla Green loves business and hates Christmas.

So when Jackson O'Neil invites her to Snow Crystal Resort to discuss their business proposal... the last thing she's expecting is to stay for Christmas dinner. As the snowflakes continue to fall, will the woman who doesn't believe in the magic of Christmas finally fall under its spell...?

4th October

www.millsandboon.co.uk/sarahmorgan

1013/MB435

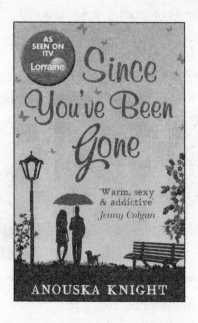

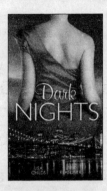
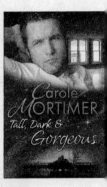